Finding
Love
Again

CHIOMA IWUNZE-IBIAM

This edition is published in 2015 by Ankara Press

© Chioma Iwunze-Ibiam, 2014
© Cover print design Vlisco

ISBN: 978-978-53151-2-7

Editor: Anthea Gordon
Production and layout: Jibril Lawal
Cover design art: Onyinye Iwu

Ankara Press:
62B, Arts and Crafts Village
Opposite Sheraton, Abuja, Nigeria
www.ankarapress.com

If you enjoyed this, you'll definitely enjoy these:

ANKARA PRESS

A New Kind of Romance

If you enjoyed this, you'll definitely enjoy these:

About Chioma Iwunze-Ibiam

Chioma is a hopeless romantic who (thankfully) studied Mathematics and Computer Science, but loves to write. Writing helps her stay sane, rational, logical and sweet. She lives in Enugu with her lawyerly husband and her pretty, hyperactive daughter. *Finding Love Again* is her first novel with Ankara Press.

Then consider becoming one of our romance writers. Just follow our submission guidelines on www.ankarapress.com. We look forward to hearing from you!

Lastly, follow us on Twitter: @ankarapress, and like us on Facebook: www.facebook.com/ankarapressbooks.

www.ankarapress.com

ANKARA PRESS
A New Kind of Romance

We you hope you enjoyed reading this book. It was brought to you by Ankara Press, an imprint of Cassava Republic Press. The more you support us, the more contemporary African romance goodness we can produce for you. Here's how you can help:

1. Recommend it
Don't keep the enjoyment of this book to yourself; tell everyone you know. Spread the word to your friends and family.

2. Join the conversation
With Twitter, Facebook, blogs and even our own website, writing a review of a book you love has never been so easy. Start a conversation about the book via your own social networking site, or discuss it with others on Goodreads.com. And don't forget to leave a comment on www.ankarapress.com.

3. Buy your own copy
Encourage your friends to buy their own copy directly from our website (rather than illegally downloading it) as copies are available with special deals and discounts for them to enjoy. Your direct purchase will enable us to continue to produce the steamy stories you just can't get enough of. Support the publishers, not the pirates!

4. Read our other racy romances
We've more where this book came from and we promise that you won't be disappointed. In fact, we know that you'll be excited at having discovered our books. Browse and buy at www.ankarapress.com.

5. Consider writing your own
Have you ever thought about writing? Do you think you can compose a compelling African romance that will leave the reader hungry for more?

left. Beba guided her as they meandered through the dancing crowd to the car park. The night sky was void of any moon and there was a scattering of stars.

All around the dimly lit park, young people stood in pairs locked in passionate embraces.

Kambi sat in the car, buckled her seatbelt, and sighed. Beba got into the driver's seat and started the car.

"Wait," Kambi said, hurriedly unbuckling her seatbelt. With his foot on the brake, Beba turned to her. And Kambi launched herself at him and kissed him full on the lips. He moaned and released his legs from the brakes. The car rolled forward. He gasped and pulled up the handbrake.

By now, Kambi was sitting on top of him, her nose sniffing his hair. He grabbed her to him and pushed his nose into her chest. He kissed her neck slowly until she cried. Then their lips met again, and they savoured each other hungrily. Their hands caressed and clung to each other.

"Not here," Kambi whispered.

Beba sighed, "You don't want us to be sued for a public display of affection?"

"Is that even an offence?" Kambi asked as she adjusted her gown and sat back in her seat.

"I think that will depend on where you are," he replied.

She grinned at him and shut her eyes. She was definitely high on something she had found on the plateau. It felt good to finally be his real fiancée.

Prologue

"With this ring, I thee wed," the priest read.

Kambi tuned out the voices of the other couples who were reciting their vows. Her head ached. Bouquet in hand, she stood at the altar in her Daisy Bridals wedding gown, confused. The ceremony was almost over and her groom was yet to arrive, as was her maid of honour.

"You may now kiss the bride," Kambi heard the priest say. Most of the congregation went wild with applause. Lifting her eyes, she stared at the other two couples with whom they'd had rehearsals. Kambi remembered the way the kisses had defined the men. The chubbier groom enveloped his bride's lips with his mouth, so that Kambi feared that he might swallow her small face. While the other groom with knees slightly bowed held his bride closely, and brushed her lips with his lips before deepening the kiss. Kambi had always hoped her groom's kiss would be the most memorable part of the wedding.

Tears welled up in her eyes. She turned backwards and saw her mother weeping into a handkerchief as Kambi's sister, Diana, consoled her. Her father sat beside their mother, frowning. His arms were folded across his sturdy chest. Kambi knew her father had never really liked Victor. But she had gone along with the marriage arrangements because, in the beginning, he'd seemed a reasonable bachelor. Perhaps she'd been too fatalistic

1

about the affair, especially with her mother harping on about the proverbial biological clock and nonsense like that.

A man, dressed in cream-coloured suit, walked down the aisle. Kambi craned her neck to see if her groom had arrived. Perhaps he had been stuck in traffic. It wouldn't be too late, she thought. They could still plead with the priest to marry them, or they could reschedule. But, as the man drew nearer, she saw that he was Victor's younger brother, the best man. She saw him whisper into Victor's mother's ear and then into Diana's. The women screamed and snapped their fingers and wailed with hands clasped behind their heads. Kambi knew then that something had gone dreadfully wrong.

Diana's twin boys – the pageboys – scuttled around the church aisle. Their mother caught them by the ears and led them to their father where he was sitting at the far end of the church. Kambi hadn't expected him to accept her wedding invitation, considering that her sister had divorced him shortly after the birth of their sons.

While the priest blessed the other couples, she dropped her bouquet, lifted the frills of her gown and ran down the aisle.

"What's going on?" she asked, dreading the worst. Why else was Victor's mother covering her face with a handkerchief, crying and saying, "I'm sorry. I'm sorry"? And why else was the best man staring at her with bashful eyes and his head tilted to one side as though he was

staring at a sick puppy? Why was he taking her aside and patting her hands?

"He's not coming," he said. Her jaw dropped. She nodded. *Life isn't over,* she thought to herself. A large tear rolled down her cheek. She wiped it off, not caring about the blusher the make-up artist had applied that morning. Her heart burned with rage and simmered with bitterness.

"Auntie Ambi, Auntie Ambi!" Diana's twins yelled. They'd bolted from their father's arms, and were scurrying towards Kambi. Most of the guests were leaving, and the church hall was getting rowdier. Kambi worried that her three-year-old nephews might not handle the crowd. But she could see their father trying to catch up with them.

Kambi turned back to the best man. "Why? Did he give any explanations at all?" she asked, and swallowed hard. It was clear that the knowledge she sought would come with its full dose of pain, so she braced herself. She imagined that knowing would erase the torture of wondering and groping endlessly in the dark for answers.

The best man shook his head and turned his face. From the side, he looked just like Victor: fair skin, shiny black beard, complete with pointed nose and thin lips.

"Oh," she said. "Have you heard from Chinwe, my maid of honour?"

He nodded. "Chinwe and ... and Victor have eloped," he stuttered.

"The slut!" Diana yelled. Kambi hadn't noticed her sister standing behind her.

Diana would have skinned Chinwe alive if she'd set eyes on her. But Kambi didn't want any more drama. Not even from her tetchy sister who was charging around like an angry bull.

The other bridesmaids huddled round her, trying to comfort her. But she didn't want to hear that everything would be fine and that Victor didn't deserve her. She knew all those things and didn't want to be reminded. Her friend Kaycee had the loudest voice. And she kept reaching out to wipe the tears that streamed from Kambi's eyes.

The sky rumbled.

Kambi removed her veil and tossed it aside. She didn't need a groom who could abandon her for her maid of dishonour. She moved away from the other bridesmaids. The twins stepped on the frills of her gown and grabbed her legs. She tripped on the frills, but didn't fall.

"You look so lovely on your wedding day!" Ayobami sang, mimicking Brenda Fassie's 'Wedding Day' hit song.

"No, she doesn't. She looks like a crybaby," Ayodeji said. They giggled. The bridesmaids had a hard time tearing the twins' hands off the wedding gown. Diana pulled their ears and led them away.

Kambi muffled her sobs as she held up her gown and started to run out of the church.

"Hold her! Hold her before she does anything rash!" her mother yelled.

Shoes made clack-a-clack-clack noises in the church as the bridesmaids hurried towards her. But she dashed out before they could reach her.

This wasn't the picture she'd had of her dream wedding since she was ten. Not like this: being chased by her bridesmaids as she ran out of the church in a bid to hide her face in shame. She hadn't imagined her pageboys singing wedding songs in bad taste. Nor had she planned to pray that the ground would open its mouth and swallow her up.

In her dreams, she was always wearing a dazzling white gown and silver shoes while her handsome groom beamed as he said his vows. But things had turned out in the worst possible way. Being a realist, she believed white gowns were for virgins – and Chinwe, her slutty maid of dishonour, had concurred – which was why she was wearing a light pink ball gown. But the colour of her gown was not as important as her inner happiness and peace.

Had she tried to settle for a man who didn't respect her? She couldn't believe that, at 24, she had almost ended up in a miserable union with a man who probably had more dark sides than she could imagine.

Kambi kept running through the church garden lined by rows of ixora and hibiscus flowers. The sky roared and darkened as she ran towards the gate. Someone called her name but she didn't look backwards or sideways. Her neck hurt. And her eyes too. Her heart was heavy with grief and disappointment and she felt exhausted.

Diana grabbed the frills of her gown. She stumbled, but Kaycee caught her by the arm so she didn't fall. "You want to get killed?" Kambi wailed. Her mother hugged her but Kambi pushed her away.

Horns blared in the distance. She heard the screeching tyres. A cacophony of sounds filled her ears. Kambi's legs weakened. The rain came down in a gentle drizzle and soaked her hair. Her head tilted up, her mouth opened. Her tongue tasted the rain.

They held her hands and led her to the car. She felt like a heifer being taken to the slaughterhouse.

Suddenly, the rain poured in sheets, washed her tears away, drenched her gown, and knocked her down on her knees.

One

To take a second chance as Victor's fiancée? No way!

Fuming at this thought, Kambi frowned as she got out of the taxi. Her jaw tightened, as did her chest. After all the pain and embarrassment he had caused her, she couldn't for the life of her imagine herself as Victor's fiancée – again. Not for all the oil wells in the Niger Delta!

It didn't matter that he had recently dumped her maid of dishonour – with whom he had eloped on their wedding day. Kambi couldn't care enough to sympathise with them, especially with all the deadlines she had to meet.

She dragged her luggage to the beautiful gate of the Obudu Mountain Resort – her temporary place of refuge. Certainly, Victor wouldn't stalk her up here. Or so she hoped, although, considering social media doesn't allow people much privacy, he could probably find her anywhere. But she imagined that he wouldn't go through the trouble of trailing her to a remote part of Cross River State. Again, she was happy that she wouldn't have to spend her days and nights at the Love 100.5 FM radio station over the next couple of weeks, presenting boring programmes and reading (or editing) depressing news items. How wonderful life would be if she could just focus on completing her collection of poetry, due for submission in two weeks. Kambi looked at her watch and sighed. In a few hours, the skies would draw their curtains. And her agent would call her to find out how her writing was going.

Completing the manuscript would bring her one step closer to her ultimate goal – to be a published author, not just a performance poet.

She raised her chin as the first lines of a poem rang in her head.

Kissing the granite-like features of that face ...
She paused.
Not the face of the uniformed guard at the gatepost,
Not the face of the nomad,
leading a herd of cattle up the hill.

Kambi shook her head like a hen shaking flies off its comb. She would have to wait until she was settled into her room. Then, she could write a poem.

For now, Kambi took in the attractions of the haven. The mountain was teeming with blogging material. From her experience, photographs helped readers connect more to her poems. This holiday was also a chance to mix work and play. Just what she had been looking for – an opportunity to escape from her chaotic life to the serenity of the Obudu Mountain Resort.

And what a tranquil, even romantic, place this was! Kambi gasped with admiration as she clicked away with her camera. Dragging her luggage past the gatepost, she photographed the sculpted cow's head, the frothing natural spring and the bright-green hills beyond. Every fibre of her being was suffused with the giddiness she felt each time she had seen commercials of the Obudu Mountain Resort on television.

A cable car conveyed her from the tropical base of the mountain up into the more temperate mountaintop. For the entire four-kilometre journey, she looked up and down at the sparkly streams criss-crossing the gorges, at the wafting clouds, and at the flowers. She breathed in the clean mountain air and decided that this trip would be more fun than she had imagined. But fun in a quiet way, which was exactly what she needed.

A travel poem about my arrival.

"How high?" Kambi asked the cable car operator. "How high is this plateau?"

She inhaled the aroma of wet grass. Rushing streams flowed around the looming slopes of the Obudu plateau and cascaded down rough black rocks. Swiftly, they flowed onto the shallow gutters that lined the narrow curve up the fog-blanketed plateau.

"About 1,600 metres above sea level," the cable car driver replied as they approached the reception

Another downward glance revealed a steel-coloured giant anaconda on the grassy plateau. Clicking away with her camera, she gasped at the impressive gorges draped with undergrowth, trees and plants, and the endless S-shaped road that slithered up the mountain.

She closed her eyes and breathed deeply. The scenery was enthralling enough to erase remnants of the haunting memories of Victor's betrayal. What a shattering experience that had been. She'd felt as though her confidence had been smashed against a wall. And, for a long time, all she had written were poems about life's complexities, forgiveness and self-preservation. She hadn't been able to trust her muse. In order to unlock more of her creative juices, she had sneaked out of Port Harcourt that morning before the first light of dawn appeared.

The sudden stop of the cable car caused her to jerk out of her reverie.

She picked up her luggage, thanked the cable operator – whose cap bore the insignia of the last mountain race competition – and stepped out into the reception.

A mask glared at her from the wall. Kambi had an eye for art. Victor had quarrelled with her over that (and most of her interests). He had such horrible taste in art, why had she agreed to marry him in the first place? She took photographs of a carving of a slouching old man leaning solemnly on a walking stick. The carving tilted slightly to the side of a bronze cow. Kambi clicked away.

"Welcome," the receptionist said, as she leaned on the marble counter. "Is this your first time here?"

Kambi nodded and read the tag on the receptionist's white cotton long-sleeved shirt – 'Mina'.

Mina stared at Kambi, as did some of the chatty men who sat on the sofa, and those who milled around the door. Kambi adjusted her jacket and caught a pair of eyes peering at her over the top of an opened Saturday *Guardian* newspaper. *It was another Saturday!*

Her phone beeped. A text message from her agent. Kambi's heart pounded faster as she responded to the message. There was real trouble: a new deadline!

Kambi wondered if everyone knew of her misfortunes. Why else were they staring? It crossed her mind that people often stared at her unashamedly. She had a small waist which she tried to conceal but to no avail. Stripper-girl figure, her friend Kaycee usually joked. Whenever she wore a belt on a long, fitted shirt and pencil jeans, she got stares, like the ones she was receiving now. Once, she had been at a book reading where she spent time discussing Rudyard Kipling's *If* with a popular poet. She had stormed out because the man kept staring at her breasts. Now, she forgot all about her agent and her mind flitted to the staring people. Why were they staring at her this time?

Flushed with embarrassment, she almost didn't hear the receptionist when she spoke.

"Nice scarf," the receptionist said, grinning. She was pointing to Kambi's turquoise scarf.

Kambi touched the cloth around her neck. She smiled shyly, her eyes registering surprise. It had been a gift from her mother. "Thank you," she said.

Kambi ran her finger down the laminated list and pointed to the chalet.

"It's not occupied at the moment," Mina said. Kambi filled in a form and looked out of the window.

Oh my God! It's him. It's Hunky Beba. She gasped and

stared with her mouth open at the tall, broad-chested mixed-race man who had once fought off hoodlums and saved her from what could have been a life-threatening attack. But that was six years ago, and Kambi wondered whether to go out and say hello or to let it pass. She chose the latter.

Every time Kambi remembered that night in her first year at the university – that night when she had been waylaid along a lonely lane on her way back from a poetry performance, after she had tripped on a stump and fallen, she wondered where Hunky Beba had come from. She had asked him, in the course of their close friendship, and he'd said, "Heaven!" Later, she learned that he was an alumnus who was at the university to process his transcript. He needed to stay on campus for a few more days because the records officers were still processing his documents.

Kambi had thought of Hunky Beba as an angel. Before he went for his masters they had spent some time together. She began to admire his smile, his eyes, his calm demeanour, his intelligence, and experience. She loved the way he treated her with respect. But she had felt so overwhelmed by emotions that she decided to end the warm friendship that they had built. She had always been the cautious kind – choosing her priorities carefully. He, too, had said he was afraid of getting hurt. Orchestrating fights and quarrels: these were her strategies for discouraging him. Once, she had turned down his invitation to accompany him to a dinner party to meet some good friends of his. It was the only way she knew how to protect herself from emotional hurt – shielding herself from love. Back then, the thought of commitment made her feel stifled, as though strong hands were gripping her throat and blocking her windpipe. Then, she was young and naïve.

Now, there was the new deadline for the submission of her poetry collection to her agent, and she just couldn't handle another distraction.

"Quite an attractive man, isn't he?"

"Who?" Kambi replied, feigning ignorance. One look at him sent shivers down her spine.

Mina raised her chin towards the window where the man was standing, staring into the sky.

Handing Kambi a sheaf of papers, Mina smiled and said, "Please sign here."

"Oh!" Kambi said with a wide smile. She signed the forms.

"No need to be shy. My half-brother has been alone a long time," Mina chattered as she pointed the remote control at the mute television in the corner. "It's good to know pretty women still find him attractive. Do you want me to hook you up?"

Bad idea. She took in Mina's oval-shaped, dark-complexioned face. Mina was a pretty girl, but she shared only one feature with Beba – the pink, plump lips. Kambi was surprised; she hadn't known he had half-siblings. She knew he was from Cross River state;

she had also learned about his time as a Peace Corps volunteer, and that he had a degree in metallurgical engineering, but she hadn't managed to learn much about his family.

"That's really nice of you," Kambi said. "But no. Thanks all the same." Kambi smiled, remembering all she had done to keep from falling for him ...

Mina sucked her teeth.

Kambi smiled and reasoned that Mina was probably an adventurous twenty-something-year-old. And, although Kambi was 24, she couldn't imagine playing love hunter.

Lately, she had been taking herself too seriously. It had taken a failed engagement, exhaustion, and a lot of cajoling from her agent for her to take a holiday. Last night, before she slept, she had decided to do something out of character: to sneak out before daylight for this trip she had been secretly planning. Her family would be furious with her.

Waiting for her keys, Kambi shivered slightly in her jacket and jeans. She looked out of the window again and he was gone. She breathed a sigh of relief. Had she made the right decision?

"Ready," Mina asked as she gave Kambi a bunch of keys. "Let me show you to your chalet."

Kambi wondered if she would run into him in the course of her stay at the resort. Was he on holiday as well? These and many other questions troubled her thoughts. Somehow, she managed to brush them aside as the double-glass doors slid open. Mina dragged her suitcase through the door and Kambi followed. A light breeze blew in their faces. A row of colourful flags billowed in the wind. A flush of relief filled Kambi and she felt unfettered, like a bird released from a cage. As they walked, Kambi counted the flags. And, when she counted the 20th flag, she took another photo and watched her steps fall in line with Mina's.

Just then, her phone beeped. A text message had come in from an unknown number.

I KNOW WHERE YOU ARE.

Two

Dinner was at the Terrace Bar and Restaurant. Kambi could have ordered a takeaway, but she wanted to see more of the plateau. She hoped to try out hiking, to learn about ranching, horse riding, and bird watching – activities that might stimulate her muse. She would do anything to make the poems flow again. As her agent had said: romantic poems filled with the mountains and birds, valleys and streams, stables and neighing horses.

Victor definitely sent that text message. I hope that the toothless bulldog won't do anything apart from bark.

She could handle this problem either by worrying or by using one of her holiday SIM cards. Kambi often inserted new SIM cards into her phone so she could contact only people she wanted to stay in touch with. She chose to use a holiday SIM. Right there in the restaurant, she brought out the card from a corner of her wallet and swapped it with the one in her phone. She sighed and muttered, "Much better."

The Obudu Mountain Resort was very cold. With a shawl draped over her shoulders, she lifted her pointed chin. Determined to forget about her concerns, she shifted her gaze from the blazing log fire at a corner of the restaurant to the dazzling chandeliers hanging from the ceiling, and then up to the elderly waiter who limped along with her tray of food.

"Hello," a man whispered behind her ear. The warmth of the man's breath, smelling of cigarettes and buttermint, tickled her skin. She shuddered. *Why did that voice remind her of Victor, her ex-fiancé? Was it just her imagination?* Startled, Kambi looked up at the tall stranger who was wearing a black suit and a bowler hat – the kind she saw politicians wearing on the news. In his large hand lay a green plastic folder.

"Hi," Kambi replied hesitantly. Suspicious, she eyed him and wondered why he was dressed as though he was headed out for a political meeting when it was 9.15pm.

"Call me Chief Kay," he said, flashing a toothy smile. Kambi tried to remember the exact words Victor had said when their mothers had introduced them. Didn't they begin with something like, "Call me ..."?

She already disliked this Chief Kay! It didn't matter what his agenda was. She had been careful to steer clear of demanding men. She hadn't come all the way up this 1,600-metre plateau to call a stranger by his ridiculous name. She could swear that she had had enough man trouble to last her two incarnations.

The grey-haired waiter hobbled towards her and laid out her dinner on the table. The jollof rice was a sumptuous tomato-red, and the grilled chicken dripped with juice. Kambi breathed in the fragrant aroma as she thanked the waiter.

Mr Kay patted his hat and stared at her. Kambi wondered if she hadn't seen him at reception.

"You're bothering me!" Kambi snapped. She glared at him, her eyebrows raised. Her tone was low and cold as the night outside. She looked up at him; the first thing she noticed was the dagger-shaped scar beside his right ear.

"Are you alone tonight?" He smiled, biting his lips through his leer.

Her eyes widened and moved down to his hands, where she noticed a wedding band. Her mouth hung open. "How is that any of your business?"

He undid the first two buttons of his shirt. Kambi frowned at his popped-up collar, at the way he rubbed the stubble on his chin.

"I like you," he said, chuckling.

Kambi sighed. That voice? Why did it make her want to yell? It sounded too much like Victor's. Pursing her lips, she willed herself to be calm. She smiled, her smile seemed mocking him.

She wanted to tell him to get lost, but she didn't want to create a scene, even though she would not be averse to it. She was generally soft-spoken and mild mannered, but she could stand up for herself.

Once she caused a rift between rival cults. That rift had turned bloody and after that she had sworn to maintain a calmer profile, especially after she had escaped being attacked. Now, she opened her mouth to spew vitriolic words. Flexing her long index finger, she turned her face and shut her eyes in a bid to control the anger welling up in her chest.

Alerted by the shrill scraping of the dining chair opposite her, she swung around. "You're bothering me. Please, go away," she said, waving him away. She did not want to open her eyes and find him sitting in front of her. She would flare up, and probably squirt pepper spray in his eyes.

She counted to three, craned her neck, and opened her eyes. Opposite her sat the light-skinned Hunky Beba: the one she had seen from the reception window, the one who had rescued her from her attackers, the same one whose friendship she had scorned. Why did fate keep making their paths cross?

Kambi gasped at the sight of his charming smile and his black, wavy slicked-back hair. It was happening again; he pulled at the strings of her heart. And she couldn't tolerate it. Not even from him, the secret object of her affection.

"Forgive me," he said. "I hope you haven't been waiting too long." He smiled and winked at her. That was the sign. They might not have remained best of friends, but they could get rid of a nuisance together.

Kambi's lips pressed together and tugged up the sides of her mouth. She played his voice over and over in her head. She used to enjoy chatting to him before the quarrels she had orchestrated. She remembered the sadness in his eyes when she had refused to attend the dinner party with him.

"No. Not so long," she said. "But where have you been?"

Mr Kay looked at Kambi and then at the handsome Beba. Kambi smiled with pride as Chief Kay muttered his apologies and slunk away. The restaurant fell quiet for a moment. Kambi held the gaze of the hunk sitting across her table. The clang-clang of falling cutlery jolted Kambi and she blinked. The hunk had won the unspoken first-to-blink contest.

What do you say to a handsome man who rescues you from a pest? Kambi thought.

They stared at each other.

"You are a good actress, Candy," he said.

"Kambi," she corrected him. He was the only person who called her by that nickname. Weirdly enough, he had called her that when he visited her the morning after that attack. 'Candy' was the first word he had said. She corrected him then, and several times during the course of their friendship. She corrected him again when she saw him at the Garden City Literary Festival in Port Harcourt and at a Book Jam session in Lagos where another argument had ensued. After her poetry performance, her sister, Diana, remarked that there was sexual tension between Kambi and the hunky man. But Kambi had quickly dismissed that insinuation.

Thank you," she said reluctantly, feeling that she should have said something less predictable. She disliked clichés.

"My pleasure. Anything for you, whom the gods keep sending my way. It hurt to see you having to listen to that salacious womaniser."

20

"How did you know he was—"

"Oh, it was obvious. The way he was leering and drooling like he could eat you up right here on your dinner table," he said, thumping his fingers on the table.

Kambi tilted her head to one side and smiled like a bashful virgin. She remembered how much she had enjoyed their conversations.

She admitted he looked more handsome than he done the last time she had seen him. Olive-complexioned as he was, he often stood out in Nigerian crowds. In the golden glare of the restaurant lights, his tanned skin shone, and his wavy hair glittered. She admired the carefree way that stray strands fell to the side of his thick curls. Occasionally, he ran his finger through the curly mass.

Shifting her weight from side to side, she recalled those moments when they had hung out at ice-cream kiosks. Back then, she had dismissed her feelings as a fleeting infatuation; nothing she allowed to grow serious enough to be admitted. She even wrote several poems about him.

It helped her manage her feelings. She stared at him and cleared her throat. Could she call him by a nickname? Hunky Beba was the nickname she'd secretly called him. She grew restless, embarrassed even. "I'll probably finish my dinner in my room," she said.

His fixed gaze excited her a little. When he narrowed his eyes and turned, she considered writing more poems about him. She watched as he motioned for the waiter to come.

The waiter smiled. "Mr Beba, we have been looking for you. The chef needs your attention in the kitchen."

Beba, Kambi thought. That's what I must call him from now on.

Beba shook her hand and disappeared into the kitchen. And, while the elderly waiter put her food in a takeaway pack, she wanted to ask him if Beba worked in the restaurant or if he owned it. But she decided against asking at all. What did his stock-in-trade matter?

Plastic bag and wallet in hand, Kambi walked out of the restaurant.

The fog was thick, a black wall almost impenetrable by light. The overhead street lamp cast a beam that brightened the haze. Because there was a fine drizzle, she couldn't see anything beyond two metres ahead. She looked into the dark, cold and quiet night and changed her mind about walking without a torch.

A strong wind howled, blowing her cream-coloured silk gown up to her waist. Shivering, she ran back into the restaurant and shut the door.

As she leaned against the wall, her eyes swept through the restaurant. People sat in twos and threes round each dinner table. Hoisting metal trays, waiters weaved expertly through the restaurant. Soft music spilled from two speakers.

She was upset with herself. She was the kind of woman who had a practical handle on things. If the visibility had been better she would have grabbed a tablemat for protection and run to her room in the rain. But the rainforest was a few metres away and it would be foolhardy of her to risk stepping on a snake. She didn't like it but she had to ask for a torch, and nicely too.

At the far end of the curtain-walled restaurant, a waiter chatted to Beba. She noted his navy-blue Etibo and her heart pounded faster in her chest. He exuded a magnificent aura that made Kambi tingle with excitement. She strode towards him, noticing how he towered over the waiter, and how the waiter made a show of lifting his head to read the man's facial expression.

As Kambi drew closer, she admired the masculinity of his broad shoulders and imagined being hugged into his broad chest. "Easy now, Kambi," she chided herself, realising she wasn't sure how to ask for a torch. She wasn't even sure what to ask for – the truth was, she could manage without an umbrella but she needed bright lights to find her way to her chalet. Watching his hair gleam in the light, she smiled. Would Beba give her a taste of her own medicine? Perhaps he was waiting for the right time. Like this moment, when she was stuck in a difficult situation ...

She composed herself and approached the waiter.

"Sir," Kambi said, tapping the waiter's shoulder.

He turned and frowned. Yellow rays bounced off his balding head.

She ignored the frown. "Can you lend me a torch? It's raining and the paths are dark. I can manage with just a torch."

Liar! Liar! Kambi upbraided herself. *Are you sure you can manage, Miss Independent? It won't hurt to ask Beba to escort you.*

She turned a sideward glance at Beba, willing him to offer his help.

"Are you leaving immediately?" Beba asked. His bright, infectious smile unsettled Kambi.

"Yes." Kambi spoke in a low, quivering voice.

"Why?" he said.

She smiled and bit her lips. *What is wrong with you, Kambi?* she chided. She steadied her feet and raised her chin to show that she was in control. Take charge, she told herself. But the waiter had already disappeared into the kitchen.

She stood erect and cleared her throat. "Do you work here now?" she asked Beba.

"Sort of. Didn't I mention I was relocating to the Obudu Mountain during one of our Facebook chats?" He smiled.

Before or after our fights? Kambi wondered.

"No, I don't remember you mentioning it." Kambi rubbed her elbow. "I imagined you were a banker now." She nodded and arranged her shawl.

He shook his head. Kambi imagined he was as averse to that kind of job as she was.

"So you're a restaurateur?" Kambi asked.

Beba shook his head. "This is my cousin's business. He's ill and so I'm helping him supervise the workers because he was expecting very important diners today.

But I do a different kind of banking. Precious stones and mineral deposits. I also recently opened a winery here," he said, searching his pockets. He pulled out a bright-green flyer and handed it to her. Kambi took the flyer, looked at it briefly and put it in her bag. She caught a hint of surprise on his face and frowned slightly. "My father's empire has always been here, though," he added.

Kambi nodded and arched her eyebrows. How much he seemed to have changed and grown. Her eyes widened in surprise, "Here? On the plateau?"

"Yes. Here. Everywhere. I grew up here. This is my hometown, my headquarters."

***

Beba thought for a moment about his mother and how little he knew about her. All he knew was that she was as hard as nails and independent like Kambi. Kambi was the kind of woman his father would want him to bring home. Hadn't he mentioned that to her? Almost as tall as him when she was wearing heels, Kambi felt tough to him. He loved her self-assuredness, her ambition. She exuded an aura that challenged him, made him dare to desire her. No-nonsense as she seemed, he decided Kambi would be worth his time.

"Are you shivering?" he asked, "Let me fetch you a jacket."

Kambi nodded with a slight frown. He was pleased. He knew she was independent and wanted to handle things on her own, but he was glad that she had accepted his offer to help.

Twitching his bushy eyebrows, he smiled. "Just a minute, please." Then he walked into the kitchen. Squaring his shoulders, he hoped he could be of more help to her. This was his chance to impress her, the way she did him. Fate had given him another opportunity to prove himself. But what if she was emotionally unavailable, like before?

Peeping from the kitchen, he observed her standing calmly by the entrance. "Beautiful," he muttered. He watched, hoping that her heart was also fluttering like a butterfly.

Three

The music changed.

Kambi closed her eyes, and swayed her head to the soft tunes of the Soweto String Quartet. The jazz music led her to imagine a waltz with Beba to the smooth melody. While they waltzed, she pictured Beba supporting her chin and kissing her. *How fatal would such an adventure be?* What if Beba kissed her, with his pink, sensuous lips? It would be sweet, warm and so ... *Don't even dream about doing something so silly.* Kambi smiled and shook her head and snapped out of her daydreaming.

No room for love until the poetry collection had been completed. She had to get her priorities right. Fulfilling her book contract was more important to her. Only a handful of poets would be remembered after they passed on and she wanted to be one of them. Again, the text from her agent had informed her of the $100,000 NLNG literary awards coming up the next year for the poetry category. The deadline was in just a few weeks' time. Much as she would have liked a brief romance in this haven, she reminded herself – as she'd taken to doing lately – of how much her dreams and hard work might be jeopardised.

Again, she shook her head. Pride wouldn't let her throw herself at a man whose advances she'd once turned down. But now she felt a stronger attraction to him. They could remain close friends, but how close was too close for comfort?

He might be a distraction, but I can balance work and love, she thought. *And who's talking about love? Good God!*

The voice in her head won the argument. She couldn't handle a dalliance!

She smoothed out the creases of her dress. Murmurs floated round the restaurant. Her heart swelled with a strange sense of joy, of hopefulness. It was unlike all the despair that had enveloped her in the past eight months, when bile and sadness had threatened to choke the life out of her.

Beba returned and handed her a brown jacket. Kambi looked into his face and admired its sheen. His big blue eyes stared back with their usual charm. She took the jacket from him. Their hands brushed. She closed her eyes for a few precious seconds in order to preserve the moment.

"Here's a torch. I brought you an umbrella, but I must warn you: it will be of little use to you." He dangled his keys. "Let me drop you off. Where are you staying?"

"In one of the new chalets," Kambi said, turning away to heave a sigh of relief.

"Nice place," he said. He was grinning now. "I'll drop you. I've closed for the day. My cousin's assistant will take over from where I've left off."

Kambi nodded.

A lady squealed somewhere in the restaurant. Startled, they looked up and saw a young man leaning over to slip a ring on the lady's finger. The stone in the ring caught a glint of light and glimmered. Kambi smiled when the newly engaged couple kissed.

"Good for them," Beba said. Then he snapped his fingers as though he had only just remembered. "I saw your wedding invitation on Facebook, about 11 months ago. Broke my heart." He let out a nervous chuckle.

Kambi frowned as she felt a knot of panic in her stomach. Memories of her engagement flooded her mind.

"Well, congrats." Beba squeezed her hand as they walked to the door. Kambi shuddered. Lines appeared on Beba's forehead. Had he got so carried away that he hadn't noticed she wasn't wearing a ring?

In anger, her mouth twisted and barked, "For what?"

"I meant, ugh," he stuttered, "congrats on the announced engagement."

Kambi paused. "The wedding, the engagement," she said, "it didn't work out."

"I'm sorry. I should have looked at your finger." He frowned again, and shook his head.

Kambi studied his new demeanour with keen interest. There was a hint of relief, a latent excitement about his reaction to her misfortune. What could that mean? Did Beba plan to make a move?

"It doesn't matter any more. I'm over it." She waved a hand to dismiss his assumption that she needed his pity. She hated to be pitied; she was a survivor. That was a better way to see it.

When she discovered that Victor had eloped with her

maid of honour, she had felt weak and worthless. With time, her loss of self-esteem affected her productivity. Now, she was becoming a pain in her agent's neck (she reminded herself to send a text message with the new SIM number). Her manager at the radio station was also getting concerned. Once, he had invited her into his office to tell her how many of their listeners had complained that she was losing her confident panache for broadcasting. And so, her boss had been happy to let her go on the much-needed holiday. Kambi hoped the process of completing the book would rebuild her confidence.

"How could he not have fought for your love? I would hold on tight, if I had you in my life. I can't imagine anyone letting you go," Beba said.

Kambi smiled and exhaled. If he knew how complicated that relationship was ... If he learned about how her groom had taken off with her maid of honour ... If only Beba knew that the runaway groom was trying to make a legendary comeback ...

Kambi pushed aside all thoughts of her past love life. She wanted so much to move on.

Huddled under the large umbrella, they strode towards Beba's car. The wind howled. She apologised and clutched his arm for support. He brushed off her apologies with a cursory 'no problem' and held her hunched shoulder. She tensed and relaxed after two steps. With each stride they took, Kambi became more convinced he was right about the near-uselessness of an umbrella. The wind blew raindrops in their faces regardless. Like drunkards, they tottered in the rain and fog.

As Kambi got into the car, the synthetic aroma of lavender air freshener struck her. "Thank you," she said.

"Mention it, please," he joked.

"What?" she asked, a little shocked and amused at his show of immodesty.

"You said 'thank you' and I begged you to mention it," he said, laughing.

"Oh." The car whined to life. His headlights bounced back the fog ineffectually. Kambi gasped, frightened by the poor level of visibility.

"I can't even see the back of my hand." She lifted her hand to her face. Turning to stare at him, she frowned in a genuine show of concern.

"It's not so bad. It's the road back home," he said, driving slowly. "I'll stick to my lane. People are civil here. No-one parks their vehicles on the side of the road."

Kambi relaxed and closed her eyes. The car rolled to a stop. He hissed and tried the ignition. The car groaned and groaned but didn't start. He kicked the brakes and apologised.

"Good God!" he said. "Must be the battery."

He opened the bonnet and bent over. Kambi looked about and remembered that night in Owerri town, how the cult boys had accosted her on that lonely lane, how she screamed herself hoarse as they dragged her down a bush path. It was almost a night like this, only not as cold. Back then, Beba had taken charge. Now, she was prepared. She felt the can of pepper spray in her bag beside the pocketknife she usually carried around with her.

Kambi got out of the car and joined him. Only the hazy headlights and the streetlamps were providing any light, so she was surprised to find him tinkering with the engine in the dimly lit street.

She fished the torch he'd given her out of her bag and switched on the light.

"Thanks for the light," he said. She nodded. Because of the cold, she had to clench her teeth to keep from chattering.

Behind the wheel again, he tried to start the engine. It whined and whined and stopped. After three tries, he gave up.

"Sorry. But we're really close. We can walk."

Kambi thought that he sounded disappointed. He muttered something that sounded like, "I should have driven the new sports car."

Kambi nodded, picked up her bag, and shut the door.

They walked along the quiet streets and listened to the cacophony of sounds from the rainforest. She was unhappy that the cold had reduced her to a mere agama lizard who could only nod. She wanted to chat but her teeth wouldn't part. It would be too embarrassing to gnash her teeth or chatter uncontrollably. She hoped he wouldn't think that she hadn't changed, that she didn't want anything more than just friendship.

They walked side by side – almost huddling together like teenage lovers – her steps falling in line with his. Kambi was uncomfortable with this arrangement because she kept stepping on his shoes. Although she apologised each time this happened, she felt annoyed with her feet. Then she realised that she was worrying too much about the thought of him judging her.

Although cold, she decided to start a conversation to take the edge off the effects of her awkward feet.

"This plateau," she said, and paused because their shoulders had brushed and he grunted something that sounded like "hmm".

"Obudu is really far from every major city in the country." She raised her voice a notch because he had slowed down and moved his head towards her.

"It's five hours from Calabar," he replied.

"More like five hours, forty-five minutes from Calabar."

"Bad roads?"

She shook her head and stepped on his shoes again. This time, Kambi patted him lightly on his back to apologise. Then, she skipped to his side.

"Actually, when we were coming, the cab driver veered off a tarred road at Ikom. Before we knew it, we were in Cameroon. Without visas or passports."

Kambi laughed, looked up, and caught his lips turning upwards into a smile. She enjoyed looking at his profile. His chiselled chin jutted out below his smooth pink lips as they pressed together and stretched up towards his dimpled cheek.

"Didn't you get stopped by the immigration officers?" he asked.

"Trust me, we just drove through the border. There was not even a single person there to stop us. I was surprised to receive a text from MTN Cameroon, welcoming me and wishing me a productive stay."

"Really?" He stretched his hands for a second.

"Yes. And even the driver got the message. So, we parked the car and asked a farmer where we were." Kambi paused and twitched her nose to suppress a sneeze.

"And the farmer said?" he prodded impatiently. Kambi imagined he was trying to picture a tall middle-aged man striding along the roads with his soiled clothes and a hoe hanging from his shoulder.

"You're in Cameroon!" Kambi said, mimicking the farmer's gruff voice. "That's what the farmer told us."

"Interesting adventure. But it's unlikely that you could have slipped into Yaounde."

"Oh well ... But what if we'd got to Yaounde unnoticed?" Kambi said.

They had arrived at Kambi's door. She clutched her bag of food and shivered as she fiddled with the keys.

"May I?" he asked as she passed him the takeaway bag.

She unlocked the door, turned, and thanked him for offering to help. Smiling, she stepped into the dimly lit living room.

"Come in, please," she said in a bid to be courteous.

***

He drew closer and put one foot in the door. Then he stopped and looked up.

"Thank you for walking me," she said.

He watched her bend over a table as she unpacked her takeaway.

"I like this place already. I wish there was a radio station here so I could live here and continue my broadcasting and spoken-word poetry." She looked up. Their eyes met. A shiver ran down her spine and she looked away.

"A transmitting station would be nice. It'd be soothing to hear your voice, every day. On the radio, I mean."

Kambi smiled.

"I should get going," he said.

"Can you find your way through this thick fog?"

"My instincts will guide me. They've never failed me."

***

A moment later, from the corner of her eye, she saw him walk back from the door into the living room and stride towards her. Her eyes widened and shut again. He held her shoulders and pressed his lips to hers in a deep, warm, lingering kiss.

Shocked into stillness, she parted her lips and opened her eyes. It was real: Beba was kissing her in her living room. A soft moan escaped from her throat. There was nothing brash or annoying about the way his lips pleasured hers. His kiss was more tantalising than it had been that one time they'd kissed in his car and she'd pushed him away. But she couldn't stop him now ... *No, stop him. Stop him! What are you doing?* the soft voice in her head cried.

She lifted up her hands in protest and then dropped them.

With both her arms resting on his broad chest, her fingers inched up slowly and locked behind his neck. The tempo rose and her body shivered. Lost in the throes of wild kisses, her mind stopped working. She didn't notice when his hands slid down her waist, didn't notice as they caressed her back.

Her hands pawed down at his muscular chest, and she leaned closer. She moved her hands up to his neck and stroked his chin. She moaned again and her hands pulled his face closer. *I'm losing myself in this ... wonderful kiss. Kambi stop, stop ... why?*

She knew that she would regret this when the kiss ended. Oh, how she wanted this kiss to never end ...

She liked the way he propped her up, the way he pulled her body closer to him as his soft lips brushed and teased hers, inviting her to savour him. It's *only a kiss, she told herself. Must it mean something?* But, this would definitely be memorable. More memorable than any kiss she'd ever had. Her knees grew weaker and she almost felt them buckling. *What a sweet, tingling sensation*, she thought as she pulled her head away.

He smiled at her, exhaled in her face and she shuddered. A magnetic force locked them together again.

Diana had to be wrong. Or had there really always been a sexual attraction between them?

Lost in her thoughts, she pinched his left ear.

"Ouch!" he groaned, stepping back.

She felt her creative muse rejuvenate. A poem could be born from this kiss.

"I'm sorry, but you have to leave," she said as she rummaged through her bag for a pen and a notepad. She felt the poem passing through her. She stamped her feet in impatience, aware of Beba's eyes on her.

Beba chuckled, "Too soon for you? Sorry, Kambi," he said.

She searched her mind for polite words to dismiss him, but she couldn't find any. They had both participated in the kiss. Hadn't they both moaned in excitement? Her jaw dropped; her eyebrows arched. The notepad was open now and she was wielding the pen in her hand.

What were the first words?

"Kambi, is everything fine? Can we sit and discuss something?"

Does he want to make a sexual proposition? Men always did that.

Her right hand waved him away. He would learn that she was a different kind of woman. And why the hell was he standing there, staring as though he was on a mission to stop her?

She sat at the table and wrote down the first two lines.

Beba walked towards her. She panicked and shut the book. Had she lost the rest of the poem?

"Ugh," Kambi's shoulders dropped in exhaustion. If the poem whizzed through her, up the mountain and down the valley, then she'd lose it.

Her creative process wasn't always like this. Sometimes she had to work doggedly to write her poems. But there were times when she had whole poems dropped into her consciousness. Those poems usually tugged at the strings of her heart.

"Am I interrupting?" Beba asked, taking her hand in his.

"Yes. Yes. Please ... " Kambi put up her hands and covered her face. "How do I explain this?"

She couldn't tell him about her book deal, nor could she tell him about her deadlines. Didn't discussing a work-in-progress bring bad luck? And what if she didn't succeed? Then, she would probably feel obliged to discuss her failure.

"You can always talk to me," Beba said. "If you ever need a patient ear, a shoulder to cry on ... "

"That's the problem!" she shouted, stamping her feet as she charged towards the door. The poem seemed to be receding and returning. She grabbed the notepad and rushed into the bedroom. As she wrote, she heard Beba asking if she was alright. She ignored him.

Five minutes later, she came out heaving a sigh of relief that the poem had come out intact.

"Are you alright now?" He smoothed her hair. She nodded slightly.

"Good! I assumed it was the food at Terrace," Beba said, holding her hand and walking to the couch.

"No. No. It's not the food. I only had a few spoons of rice. I'm fine."

"Are you sure?"

"Of course I'm sure!"

"Alright, then. Here's my number." He handed her a business card. "Keep in touch, please." He felt her temperature with the back of his hand. "You need to rest. Good night."

He thrust his hands in his pockets and left the house. She locked the door behind him.

She leaned on the door and listened to his footsteps dissolving into the quiet, foggy night.

She bit her lip and reflected on the kiss they had just shared and the poem she had written. Then she noticed he'd left his jacket resting on the back of a chair. She looked at the business card he'd pressed into her palm.

Kambi liked the way he made her feel. But she hadn't forgotten how much it hurt to open up oneself to a rush of pleasurable emotions. Hadn't she decided she wouldn't get involved with any man just yet?

Kambi wondered if she could have her cake and eat it too? Just a holiday treat, which would end soon?

No, she wouldn't be swayed by the irresistible Beba.

Four

Beba tossed and turned in his bed, thinking of Kambi. He remembered that night when he had first seen her perform her poetry. He remembered her witty introductory speech. He had known that she was intelligent, funny, and strong-willed. She wasn't like any girl he'd ever met. He remembered how dazed he had been to see her at the Terrace Bar and Restaurant. His heart somersaulted in excitement as his mind replayed their past conversations. He gave up trying to sleep and walked to the kitchen.

He set a kettle of water to boil and put a bag of green tea in a mug. Her face flashed in his mind. He paused and daydreamed of the softness of her lips and her gentle caress. His hands ached for her supple body. He wished she were there with him, so that he could hold her close to him.

The whistling kettle jolted him out of his reverie. He turned off the cooker and poured the water into the mug. The rising steam warmed his face and he remembered how tired he was, having spent his whole day working at his business and then supervising his cousin's restaurant in the evening. But meeting Kambi made it all worth it.

He sipped his tea and hoped that he would be able to get up at 5.30am. He always started work at 6.30am. That had been his routine since he set up Kems Industries – a conglomerate of mining companies, a vineyard and a winery – on the Obudu plateau. He could have set up his enterprise anywhere in the country, but Obudu was home and its serenity soothed his soul.

Lately, he had been planning to embark on the search for his mother – a South African woman named Marie whom his father once loved. Beba had searched online and even employed the services of a private investigator, but to no avail. When he finished his masters programme, he returned home, expecting the search to be easier. But things hadn't worked out as planned. His father had proved tougher than expected.

Marie had made his father swear – and Beba didn't know why – that he wouldn't disclose her location until Beba had brought home a bride-to-be. It had never made sense to him, except perhaps when he overheard his father discussing Marie's battle with clinical depression. Twice, Marie had slit her wrists, after which she had lain in the bathtub almost bleeding to death. Each time, the same events followed – a Sunday evening, the same bathtub, the same knife. They were both undergraduates at the University of the Witwatersrand and Beba's father had hoped that his love for her would save her.

Beba sipped his tea. He was concerned about Marie. Was she alive and well? Or had she killed herself? He shuddered at the thought of never knowing her. Deep in his heart he loved her, even though he had never met her.

Beba imagined that she had been traumatised by the circumstances of his birth. His courageous father had needed to sneak out of apartheid South Africa with their mixed-race baby. Was Marie scared that Beba would run back to her when he wasn't mature enough to understand? Perhaps she had not envisaged that the apartheid system would end. Beba was still trying to wrap his mind around the strangeness of it all.

He set his mug on the reading table, and put on the lamp. His gaze fell on the feasibility studies, risk management reports and cost plans for the new brand of red wine they planned to introduce into the market. Reading the reports, he sipped his tea and made notes. Given the size of the population, the market was viable, especially with the bad reports other brands of alcohol were getting. Yet, this business had other challenges.

Kambi crossed his mind again. He closed the file and drank his tea. He remembered the night of their meeting on campus. Bernice, his girlfriend, had just broken up with him and he was soon to leave for his masters degree in Europe. He'd been organising for his transcript to be sent to the universities he'd applied to. Kambi was aware of all the drama in his life, so they stayed platonic friends and nothing more. The brief kiss they had shared meant a lot to him, even though she had pushed him away.

Back then, he been surprised at his hopefulness and excitement. In the first phase of their friendship, he had been so crazy about her that he had asked that they start a relationship.

But she had resisted him, insisting that they remained

friends. He understood that she wanted to concentrate on her studies and wouldn't compromise. Even the kiss couldn't change her mind. Though it hurt, he saw that she didn't want to mix up her priorities. He hadn't had any serious relationships since. He'd tried to date a couple of times, but things hadn't quite worked out.

Now, he considered the possibility that Kambi might give them a chance. Or perhaps she might help in his search for his mother. Would she agree to be his pretend fiancée? His father and stepmother would see that he was clearly in love with her intelligence and beauty.

His whole being craved Kambi's company, for reasons he couldn't fathom. He genuinely wanted to see her as soon as the first light of dawn appeared. But how could he knock at her door so early in the morning? What if she misinterpreted his intentions and told him to get lost? He finished his tea and went to bed. He would sleep on it and the solution would pop into his mind, he hoped.

***

Beba was clutching his pillow and mumbling Kambi's name when the alarm clock rang. He jumped up from his bed, sweating profusely. He'd been dreaming about Kambi.

He squinted his blurry eyes, wiped them with the back of his hands. Walking to the bathroom, he slapped his forehead. He had two meetings today. It'd be a miracle if he was able to concentrate enough to get any work done.

Freshened up and dressed in a shirt and tie, he arrived at the office building at about 6.30am.

"Good morning, sir," his secretary said, stepping up to him.

"Good morning, Lillian," he replied. He walked past her and into his office.

He sat behind the huge mahogany desk and looked at his diary for the day. He had to get through two meetings with prospective clients. He had just opened the bids for contracts when Lillian came in to remind him of his first meeting at 7.15am. He nodded and glanced at his diary.

"And the second meeting is at 11.30?"

"Yes, sir," Lillian said, nodding. She cleared her throat and adjusted her skirt.

"Should I bring you coffee or tea, sir?" she said. *Bring me Kambi,* his heart replied.

"Nothing. I'm fine," he replied, waving her away.

"Sir, today is a public holiday."

"Really?"

"Yes, sir. Could we have a half-day off?"

"I'll have to think about it," he said, wondering what he'd be doing at home afterwards. Dreaming of Kambi?

Lillian interrupted his thoughts again. "Sir, are you alright?" she asked. "Your eyes are ... did you get enough sleep?"

"Lillian, go and get the conference room ready for the first meeting," he barked.

She shut the door behind her. Beba sighed and leaned

back in his chair. His jacket, he thought. Kambi still had his jacket. He could visit her under the pretext that he wanted to retrieve it. *Bingo!*

Smiling, he drummed on the table and muttered a victorious "Yes!"

He would visit her, immediately after the first meeting. The second meeting would have to be cancelled. Dialling the intercom, Lillian answered at the other end of the line.

"Call the other contractors to cancel the second meeting, and reschedule," he said.

"Yes, sir."

"And you can all go home after the first meeting. Happy holiday."

He heard Lillian yelp in excitement as he hung up the intercom.

Five

The purple silk negligee slid off Kambi's slender shoulders and dropped around her ankles as she hummed a soulful song. She stood at the bathroom door, wondering where the song had come from.

The ringing phone jarred her back into consciousness. She cupped her breasts, and ran. Snatching her phone from the small bedside table, she clicked the receiver button.

"This is Kambi, The Love Goddess," she joked. Love Goddess was her signature for a night programme she ran for Love 100.5 FM.

"Kambi, why didn't you call to say that you'd arrived? And you switched off your regular phone! Why have you been ignoring my e-mails?"

"Tima! But I sent a text message with my holiday number!" Kambi exclaimed. It was the last thing she'd done before she went to bed; she'd sent the text message to Tima and Diana. She could have sent messages to her parents, but she wasn't ready to start speaking with her mother. Her father, on the other hand, had been mediating between Kambi and her mother.

Kambi breathed deeply. These days, the sound of her agent's voice caused her heart to skip two beats.

"Relax," Tima said. "How is Obudu this morning?" Kambi sighed.

"A little wintry," she replied, flipping through her notepad. She'd written two poems since her arrival, but she couldn't tell her agent that. Tima would fly off the handle if she knew that was all Kambi had produced.

"Winter? In Nigeria?" Tima asked. Kambi frowned at the hint of sarcasm in Tima's voice.

"Yeah. Here, there are four seasons each day. Winter at dawn, Spring mid-morning till noon. Summer in the early afternoon and rain in the late afternoon. And the nights are ... "

"Kambi, you haven't been there a full day yet. Anyway, have you completed half of the project?" Tima queried in her husky, businesslike voice. Born into an aristocratic family, she was rich and independent and unmarried. No-one knew why she'd chosen to go the literary agency and publishing route. It was no secret that Tima could be ruthless when it came to business.

Kambi's jaw dropped. "Er," she groaned, "I wrote a few poems last night, in spite of my exhaustion."

At the other end of the line, Tima rapped on the desk as she was in the habit of doing whenever she was under pressure. Kambi braced herself.

"I know you're doing your best but the Publisher I want to submit your collection to is filling my head with a lot of yak about how spoken-word poets are wonderful for stage performances, not as authors. I don't believe her but I'm afraid."

Kambi interpreted that to mean her reputation was at stake.

"I'm working very hard on the drafts. You know all I have been through. Which reminds me; I met this great guy from my past last night. But I can't give him a chance because of this project," Kambi rambled.

"Wait," Tima said, breathing into the phone. "You met someone you like? That's great news. Write a poem about every exotic date you go on." Kambi could hear her banging the top of her table.

"Why?" Kambi whispered. "We agreed that staying away from love interests would help me concentrate ... "

Kambi could hear her chuckling in between intermittent slurps of her morning coffee.

"But it's been eight – or ten – months since you and that Victor guy parted ways. You haven't written a single joyful poem ever since. You know the requirements: we need happy and romantic poems."

"What I need is a break from the hassles in my life. Not a man. My poetry is an outlet for me – I don't want to call it a catharsis, though sometimes it is. But, I don't need a love interest to be inspired," Kambi said. Sweat trickled down her neck. She picked up a magazine and fanned herself.

"Think about it, last night, you met that guy – what's his name? And you wrote a few poems. Somehow, I think a person's writing can change when something new happens in their lives. Am I making any sense?"

Kambi sighed.

Tima continued, "Now, I'm hopeful and it's because of that guy ... "

The whinny of a horse drifted into the room, and she got up to look. She tipped the blinds and shrouded in the morning mist was a man sitting astride a clopping, chestnut horse.

"You have gone quiet. Is someone at your door?"

"I have to go." Kambi replied, "Network is – bad. Hello, hello! I can't hear you."

"Hang up if you want. But I think you should enjoy this new experience. I'm not saying dating him is the only way you'll gather genuine materials for romantic poems. But, do your best," Tima pleaded. Her voice had risen an octave.

"Noted," Kambi said.

"Alright, go get your man. Bye." Tima hung up before Kambi could protest.

The same soulful tune continued to play in Kambi's head. She tried to shake off the song as she tipped the blinds again and watched the man jump down from the horse. "Beba," she whispered. In the soft morning light, his tanned skin glowed. He bent over to tie the horse to a short pine tree. Then he looked up and their eyes met.

"Oh my! What the hell?" Kambi muttered, brushing the blinds with her hands as she closed them. Her heart pounded faster in her breast.

I hope he didn't see me naked.

Kambi strapped on her bra, talking to herself as she scurried about. "Horrible! Indecent of me; not a good way to start off a friendship."

In the bathroom, she squirted a gloop of toothpaste and

filled her glass with water from the tap. That was when she heard the gentle knock on her door.

"Hurry," she whispered to the girl in the mirror. She heard another knock.

"Hurry," the girl in the mirror mouthed. She narrowed her bright, brown eyes. Her small face glimmered. Her nose stood long and pointed like a sculpted feature. People often said her nose was her best attribute but she liked her pouty, warm-chocolatey lips better.

Kambi rinsed her mouth and dashed out of the bathroom. She slipped on her panties and a robe. Looking down at her knees, she decided the robe was too short and wished she had packed pyjamas.

The low persistent knock caused a knot to form in her stomach as she pulled a big white T-shirt over her blue jeans.

"Coming!" she yelled.

Kambi unlocked the door.

He towered over her in the doorway. Startled, she looked at his wide eyes flecked with specks of red veins. He tucked his hands into his jeans pockets. Now, Kambi could get a glimpse of his narrow waist. His fitted shirt was neatly tucked into his jeans, revealing his exquisite build. In the morning light, Kambi saw his toned muscles. He stared back at her.

"Bad timing?" he asked. "I'm sorry."

Kambi shook her head and waved away his apologies.

"I should be apologising for keeping you waiting.

Come in and sit."

Beba walked into the living room. "I hope you had a good rest."

"Yes, I did, thank you," Kambi replied.

They stood silently staring at each other.

"You forgot your jacket," she said, picking it up from the couch to hand it to him.

Beba took the jacket from her and a cold wind rippled through the blinds. They sat down on the couch and she thanked him again for walking her to her chalet the night before.

"Oh, mention it," Beba replied. They remembered the joke they'd shared the night before and let out raucous peals of laughter. Kambi couldn't recall the last time she'd laughed so hard. A weight lifted from her chest.

Kambi felt as though his penetrating gaze bored holes in her skin. Shifting in her seat, she cleared her throat. Beba smiled.

"I really need to talk to you about something," he said. "But that will be later."

Rising from his seat, he turned around and left the chalet. Kambi's curiosity got the better of her. Part of her wanted to be left alone to write, but the other part wanted him to hold her and speak to her. Kambi held the door ajar, watching as he walked towards his horse.

The fog was dissipating. Clouds of mist wafted over the garden, where Beba crouched beside the pine tree, untying the harness.

"Excuse me, Bee," she called, wondering where that nickname had come from.

Beba turned. Kambi thought that he looked strangely quiet and unhappy. But she didn't want to pry. Her journalistic instincts were getting the better of her.

"I was thinking of walking around. Perhaps, to the stable and to see the cows," she paused, "Could you introduce me to a good tour guide?"

Beba stood with the leather in his hand.

"Today is a public holiday. I'm not sure most of the tour guides will be very busy. I would take you but I have a busy schedule," he said. Pulling out a small diary from his back pocket, he stared at her. Kambi looked away. She liked men with busy schedules, especially men who made time out in spite of those schedules.

"Don't worry about it then," Kambi started to say. She batted her eyelids in resignation.

"But I could come by at noon. Would you be ready by then?" he asked.

Kambi paused and nodded.

"I'll see you then," Beba said. He jumped onto his whinnying horse, touched the rim of his hat and nodded.

With her mouth open, she raised her hand and waved.

She went back to the chalet and shut the door. She stood at the window and watched the horse galloping away with its rider until they both disappeared into the fog.

Beggars couldn't be choosers. She would have preferred a tour guide, but if none was available then she had to oblige the man whose smile mesmerised her. Perhaps Tima was right.

She called the receptionist's office. The lines were busy. She dialled again but to no avail. She switched off her phone after the fifth try and banged it on the table. Rising from the sofa, she went to get ready for her outing.

Six

Beba arrived on his horse just as Kambi was considering Kaycee's fashion advice. Kaycee, her friend, was a confirmed fashionista. She had made the gowns the bridesmaids wore to the botched wedding. Kambi was proud of Kaycee's clothing designs, but she didn't always agree with her advice.

"Wear a swimsuit. A sexy one," Kaycee said.

"A swimsuit? To the ranch? And the stable? Why?" Kambi asked.

"Yes. Kambi, listen," Kaycee continued. "There are lots of mountain pools and springs there. Who knows?"

"I don't know," Kambi said, peeking out of the blinds. She saw Beba looking at his watch. "Oh my God, he's here."

"Who, Mr Hunk? Relax. Wear a brightly coloured shirt over the sexy swimsuit. A pink shirt will be perfect." Kaycee's voice was thinner now.

Kambi put the phone on loudspeaker mode.

The neighing of the horse wafted into the room as Kambi slipped into the swimsuit.

"I can't believe I'm giving you fashion advice for free when you didn't even tell me you were passing through my own town! You know I am still living in Calabar, yet ..."

"I'm sorry," Kambi said. "I've put on my shirt. I'm wearing a pair of jeans now."

"Are they blue?"

"Yes!"

"Good!" Kaycee said.

There was a series of loud knocks.

"Don't panic," Kaycee said. "So you have a new boyfriend?"

"He's not my boyfriend," Kambi retorted as she put on her hiking boots.

"Lucky you," Kaycee continued as though she hadn't heard Kambi's protestations. "I haven't been so lucky. My Tonye has been acting strangely, but I don't want to bother you with our problems. What's the worst that can happen, eh? We'll break up if it gets unbearable," Kaycee concluded with a long sigh.

Kambi rolled her eyes. How many times had Kaycee used that line? Kaycee had been with Tonye since their first year in the University of Calabar. They would quarrel, kiss, break up and make up. Kambi had got tired of hearing about their quarrels and had told Kaycee to discuss them with Diana instead.

"Everything will be fine, Kaycee," Kambi said. She swung her twists from side to side. "My hair ..." she said, spritzing her scalp with her home-made moisturiser of water and coconut oil.

"Put your hair up," Kaycee said. "And have fun. Open your heart."

Kambi remembered the text message. *Should I tell Kaycee about the strange text message? I should tell someone at least. Well ... I can't now, as the line is breaking up.*

"Bye," Kambi said. She put on her black, wide-brimmed hat and hung up.

The mirror reflected a ranch administrator. Kambi winked at her image and smiled. Walking to the living room, she tossed her phone, writing pad and pen, lip gloss, pepper spray and wallet in a small bag.

She opened the door and found Beba standing in the doorway.

"Hi, I'm sorry I'm late again," she said. He was standing at the threshold now. His eyes were clearer and brighter than they had been earlier in the morning.

She hurried back, leaving the door ajar. Slivers of sunlight filtered into the living room, darkening his face with patches of shadows.

"I'm always on time," he said and smiled.

He stepped back and regarded her. Kambi shifted her weight from one leg to the other. She felt his eyes boring holes in her skin. She folded her arms across her chest and began to walk around him until he laughed.

"You look like a gorgeous ranch executive," he said, smiling.

"Can we go now?" she asked, grateful to Kaycee for helping her pick appropriate attire for the ranch tour.

"Of course," Beba said, as he left the chalet.

While Kambi locked the door, he untied the horse. She struggled to extract the key from the lock. From the corner of her eye, she saw him watching her. And when he asked if she needed a hand she shook her head and pulled out the key.

She strode towards him, where he was already straddling his horse. Kambi put more action into her striding. With each step, she landed on her toes, swinging her hips and shaking imaginary locks away from her face. Her heeled hiking boots gleamed in the midday sun, as she stood tall and confident beside the horse. Hands in her pockets, she stood and smiled.

"Are we touring on the horse?" There was a hint of sarcasm in her voice.

"The horse? I call him Manny," Beba replied, squinting, "and yes, we will tour on the horse. You'll get a better view when you're sitting on Manny's back. My car broke down last night. You know the story. There's another car but like I said ..."

"I'll get a better view when I'm sitting on Manny's back," Kambi broke in. Holding her hand up in surrender, she sighed, "OK. Cool." Placing a hand on the horse's back, she put her left foot in the stirrup iron and mounted the horse. He followed and sat behind her.

"You'll ride?" he said.

She threw her head backwards and laughed. "I rode a horse once on Lekki beach. I'm not sure that qualifies me to ride one unaided," she said.

"There's always a first time, or a second," he said softly. Kambi frowned and peered at his face out of the corner of her eyes. She felt like an Amazonian warrior straddled on the fine horse with a potential lover. Kambi sighed. The first time she had ridden a horse, she'd been with her sister, Diana. They screamed in excitement as they rode; she clutched Diana's shirt while Diana pulled the harness. What an exhilarating experience that had been. Now, she was expecting it to be even better. Kambi sighed as Beba guided her hands to pull the harness.

The horse neighed and galloped; she laughed and clutched Beba's hand.

Seven

While Manny trotted along the plains, Kambi got a better view of the surrounding mountaintops, which were swallowed up in the cloudy horizons. She savoured the lush greenery of the meadows and valleys, and the life of the mountain inhabitants.

On one field, excited children chased two dogs, a couple held hands as they climbed a knoll, and a lady wearing braids waved as she cycled past them.

Beba pulled the reins and Manny stopped. Kambi and Beba alighted.

"Welcome to the mountain stable," Beba said. She nodded and looked around the bright-green meadow. A young man walked up to them.

"Welcome. Come in." He beckoned, opening the gatepost. They went in.

The man was wearing blue jeans with a cross strap design on the back. His straw hat, wide as an umbrella, shielded his bearded, brown face. He smelled of hay and horses.

"Bem, this is Kambi, an old friend of mine. She's a broadcaster holidaying here," Beba said. "Kambi, Bem is my cousin. He works here in the stable, caring for the horses."

Kambi nodded and responded to his greetings. "Pleased to meet you too," she said. Bem shook her hand

and turned to Beba. They began to chat in Utugwang and Kambi batted her eyelashes wondering what they were talking about. Looking away, she focused on the horses. She was Igbo, so she couldn't speak or understand Utugwang. And she'd never travelled to the northern part of Cross River state, where people from many different ethnic groups had settled. There were so many languages here; Kambi imagined she'd have to become a full-time linguist – not a simple poet – to grasp them all.

Tuning out the men's voices, she watched the horses as they moved about with their heads bowed over the grass in sad repose. Manny moved among the other horses as though he was making rounds to greet old friends.

Beba touched her shoulder and led her into the stables, which were clean and smelled of fresh hay. Kambi listened as Bem explained the lifespan of the horses and their reproductive health. Their feet crunched the needles of hay as they walked around, inspecting the horses.

Kambi gently touched the oldest horse on its head.

Before they left, Bem said, "Beba, you should bring her to the party tomorrow night."

Kambi was confused.

"Well, we'll talk about that later," Beba replied, half-heartedly. He walked away.

Bem stood in front of Kambi. "Promise," he begged, "promise you'll accompany Beba tomorrow night?"

"Beba can ask a woman out on a date himself," Kambi said. She turned to Beba, arching her eyebrows.

Kambi loved the way Beba watched her; his eyebrows were arched too. His pink lips spread in a quiet smile as though he planned to take her up on her challenge. *Am I giving him ideas?*

"What time is this party?" she asked.

"Tomorrow at 7.30pm," Beba said.

"It'll be lots of fun ... a bonfire," Bem added, clasping his hand in a plea. Kambi exhaled, turning to Beba.

"Would you like to go with me?" Beba asked. "I could arrange for you to give a poetry performance."

"That will be great. But I'd like to get back to my room before 10.30pm."

"Alright then," Beba said as he walked towards the stable. A series of tongue clicks brought Manny trotting towards him.

Beba doffed his hat to Bem. Kambi frowned at him, wondering what secrets they'd shared in the mountain language. And why had his cousin concluded that she would make a perfect date for Beba?

She raised her chin and looked at Beba. Their eyes locked. He shifted his gaze. Standing next to the horse against the grey sky he looked like a black and white painting, thought Kambi as she mounted the horse and sat on the saddle.

She relaxed when his fingers clasped her palms. She felt his broad chest press against her back like a shield. When was the last time she'd felt this ... safe? It was soothing to be so close to him and to have his warm hands hold her.

61

How would she begin a poem about riding on a horse with a lover?

They rode in silence. Kambi was lost in her thoughts, her eyes shut in a reverie. Until she felt Beba's grip tighten around her waist, his hands tighten on her. The horse neighed, halted and reared up.

Kambi yelped. Her eyes flew open to reveal huge cows milling all around them.

"Shoo! Go away!" Kambi yelled, waving the cows away. "What do we do?" she asked, kicking at them and reaching for the spray in her bag.

"Relax!" he said.

She took a deep breath. The air smelled of wet grass, cow dung and milk.

"Unconventional material for prose-poetry," she muttered to herself, breathing out.

On the previous night, she'd blogged about her experience in the cable car and the weather and the restaurant. Tonight, she would be happy to frighten her readers with what she considered a near-death experience. She only hoped they wouldn't end up in a hospital ...

Beba tried to pull Manny around, but the horse wouldn't budge. "I really don't want to whip you, Manny." But the intimidating cows were mooing loudly and shoving Manny aside.

"Wow!" Kambi cried out. Manny neighed as Beba pulled the reins.

"Move, move Manny. Where are the cattle rearers?"

Beba bellowed, whipping Manny lightly. He steered Manny away from two bulls close by. More cows had surrounded them by now. Kambi kicked the air to scare the cows away. Kambi tried to think of a more heroic way to rescue them from the herd of giant cows. What a good opportunity to save them both from a catastrophe. Suddenly, she saw the Fulani nomads running towards them with their sticks. Kambi beckoned to them with her hands.

"Hey! Control these cows!" Beba shouted.

Holding Kambi's shoulders, Beba whispered, 'Be calm' in her ear.

Kambi responded, "I am fine."

She imagined a real disaster where one of the cows drove its horns into Manny's side and he fell over, while Beba held her in his arms.

The Fulani's yells and whiplashes shook her out of her reverie. Waving their sticks, they restored order and the cows moved away from the tarred road. Kambi heaved a sigh of relief. Beba hugged her and said, "I hope you're OK." She nodded in affirmation. She felt closer to him.

As she turned to look at Beba, their eyes met. Kambi threw her head back and laughed. Tears glistened in her eyes.

"That was fun. Oh dear!"

Beba smiled. They continued and stopped again a few metres from the dairy farm. There they bought some bottles of yoghurt and rode on in silence. Stopping at the gatepost, they secured Manny's reins and, carrying their lunch, they walked passed the gatekeeper into the cave. This wasn't very hard to do. Beba only had to doff his hat to the gatekeeper and to greet him cheerfully and the man was too happy to care about the parcel wrapped in a plastic bag.

When they reached the grotto, she gasped at the sparkling spring gushing forth from the rock. Awed by the ferns and moss creeping all over the surrounding rocks, she clutched Beba's arm. He led her across to sit on a dry rock at the side of the pool. They sat in the shadows of the looming trees, dangling their feet in the water. Whipping out her notepad, Kambi scribbled a short poem. Beba sat beside her, unwrapping their food. There seemed to be an unspoken agreement and understanding between them: they both knew when the other needed personal space.

"This place is magical," Kambi said. She looked up and squinted at the mild rays of sunlight dancing on tree branches and leaves. Birds fluttered their wings and sang discordant tunes.

"I used to come here a lot during school holidays," Beba said.

Kambi looked at him and smiled. Two small lines appeared on her forehead.

"What was it like," she asked him, "growing up here on the mountain?"

Beba sighed.

"It was ..." he said. "It was OK. Nothing special. I felt at peace and in tune with nature. But things changed when I got obsessed with the search for my mother." He handed her a bottle of yoghurt.

"Do you know where she is?"

Beba shook his head. "I have a vague idea. But I know that my father knows." He took another swig of his yoghurt.

"Deep stuff," Kambi said. She tried to imagine his grief but couldn't. Her mother's love was given her at no cost; it had always been a prerogative she took for granted. For the first time since the botched wedding, Kambi thought of her mother in a different way. Her mother had always been supportive and loving, until their bond became strained by the shame the arranged marriage had brought.

Kambi tilted her head to one side. From the corner of her eyes, she took in his sad demeanour and shuddered. It had never really occurred to her that a man as rich and handsome as Beba could experience such a depth of sadness.

"There were many lonely days." He paused and sighed. "Let's talk about something else, like ... why don't you tell me what happened with your engagement?"

"Why?"

"Because I am concerned. You know my secret, now tell me yours." He looked away at the shallow pool.

"There's no secret. Bad things happen. Our actions are a function of our characters and free will. It's a long story," she said. The sad truth about the story was not so much its length, as the sickening idea that Victor had eloped with her maid of dishonour.

Then Kambi added: "He's trying to come back. It's over for me. He's a joker really."

"Who? Your ex? Do you want him back? Are you going to let all this chemistry between us go to waste?" he asked, touching her shoulder.

Kambi shook her head and punched his arm in a playful manner. "What chemistry?" She enjoyed the desperation in his voice.

"Don't pretend you can't feel it." He leaned towards her.

Kambi felt his breath on her neck. She shut her eyes and counted in her heart. One. Two. Three. His lips brushed hers. She shivered, opened her eyes and pulled away. "Oh my God," she whispered, turning her face.

"What is it? Are you still in love with him?" he asked. He nibbled her ear with his teeth.

"No," she said. "It's not that." Her chest was heaving now; her breathing was noisy. She could hear a cautionary voice in her head saying quite loudly: *You have to control your emotions. If you don't keep them in check, you'll risk misplacing your priorities or making another mistake.*

"Then what?" His voice was gentle. Slowly, he stood up and walked towards the spring and back. "Perhaps you aren't ready?"

Kambi searched his face. He's so tactful, she thought. She had always admired him for his level-headedness. Kambi had a weakness for men like him.

She sighed and gulped the last drop of her yoghurt.

"Beba, betrayal isn't easy to forget. The man took off

with my maid of dishonour on our wedding day." Kambi's voice was low and calm.

Beba looked into her eyes: "Maid of dishonour indeed," he said. Raising his index finger, he added, "Were there signs?"

"Only a premonition. Nothing concrete. Our mothers introduced us," she said, shrugging her shoulders.

"Your mothers?"

"I know. I know. I can't believe it myself," Kambi said, chest heaving. "It's against everything I stand for, but I was raised to believe that family is my first duty. I swear, I'll never consider it again, ever!"

She glanced at the pool. The spring was said to have healing powers. But no-one had proven it to Kambi yet. She wanted her heart and soul to be healed of all the hurt, pain and shame she bore.

She said a silent prayer as waves rippled through the water and sparkled in the mild sunlight.

***

Beba thought about it for a while. He considered her too pretty to end up in an arranged marriage. How difficult could it be for a woman as attractive as Kambi to find someone? He wondered how her mother would assume that she didn't know what she wanted in a man. Kambi, who had graduated one of the best in her class – and had spent years writing and performing her own poems – couldn't possibly be so clueless.

But he knew how difficult it was to find genuine love, having searched his whole life without success. Occasionally, he'd agreed to go on blind dates, which often went awry. Once, he went on a date with a lady who was so dim and vain, the only thing she cared about was celebrity gossip.

Now that fate had brought Kambi his way, he was glad to enjoy the company of a smart woman. Why else did his heart gravitate towards Kambi? She had been through a lot and had to be treated with care and patience.

A bird's dropping landed on his arm. He shuddered and dropped the half-empty bottle of yoghurt on the ground. Kambi laughed. Beba stared at her. He loved her high laughter; it made him feel like a boy.

They laughed so hard that their eyes sparkled with tears. Beba restrained himself from reaching out to wipe her tears. He watched her shoulders shudder with happiness. And he was thankful for the gift of her company. Their voices echoed off the walls of the surrounding trees and rocks. For a brief moment, they enjoyed this world they'd made theirs, this world they inhabited. It was theirs alone.

Beba held her gaze and she held his. It was magical, this art of staring, unblinking.

Beba had never looked into a woman's eyes like this before. He felt at once that he should preserve the moment; put it on pause with a remote control. His heart pounded against his chest as he reached out and touched her jaw. Kambi's eyes closed instinctively. He leaned over, brushed his lips against hers. She sighed, reached out and cupped his face in her hands and kissed him. He didn't resist her.

They paused and he whispered her name in her ear. "I can't explain the effect you have on me," he said, nibbling her ear. She shivered, smiled, and moved away.

"Don't run away again," he said, depositing feathery kisses on her cheeks, her chin, her nose, and forehead. She exhaled in his face. He drew in her sweet breath and leaned over. Warm, moist, and hungry lips melted into each other. His left hand supported her back as her hand combed his curly hair. They moaned in unison as the patches of sunlight danced on their faces.

Beba pulled her close until her breasts pressed against his chest. His heart swelled with longing, as she returned his kisses with as much passion. His loins awakened with a new life. He groaned. His fingers dug behind her jeans, felt the tightness of her belt. Her upper torso stiffened at his touch, yet he pressed his lips on hers. His heart broke as her hand pushed him away. It took him a great deal of strength to hold back. He willed himself to have the courage to respect her wishes to stop.

Eight

She bowed her head and gasped. "Stop," she said. It came out as a raspy whisper. He held her chin up and looked into her eyes. The intensity of his gaze caused a stirring in her. The warmth of his breath was on her face. Their foreheads touched. "This is—"

"Magic," he cut in.

"No," Kambi said, laughing. She turned her face to the spring, fixing her eyes on the ripples. "I should leave." She couldn't afford to let the tempo rise any higher. Not just yet. She reminded herself that there was work waiting to be attended to. I can't compromise work for a casual romance, she thought.

She stood, wondering how readers of her blog, *Diary of a Jilted Bride,* would react when she blogged about this kiss. Would Beba read her blog? Would she write a sincere poem? Perhaps, she thought, feeling surprised about how happy the kiss made her feel. Her heart felt like a bird, soaring sky-high, wild and free.

Beba pulled her into his arms; she leaned forward, stopped, and pulled back. Like a game between two confused pre-teens, they pushed and pulled until Kambi surrendered and fell into his arms. They pulled their hiking boots off and waded into the stream. Cool water lapped around their ankles. He turned and stared into her eyes; an intense stare that forced her mind to shut out every doubt. She concentrated on being there, alone with him in the secluded grotto, yearning for another magical kiss. In anticipation, she closed her eyes. Slowly, her guard disintegrated like a wall coming down.

She parted her lips to speak, but the words didn't come out. Her head swirled and swirled. She felt powerless, even as his hand rested on the small of her back. As he drew her further into the water, her breasts pressed into his muscular chest. She wanted him, had always wanted him. Why had it taken her so long to admit it? Was it a function of fear? Or a factor of pride? It didn't matter. Being so close to him, seeing him flush pink in the pool under the mild afternoon sun, caused her heart to race.

What was taking him so long, she wondered. She opened her eyes just as his lips brushed against hers. She pushed him away; her moment's passion was waning now. She could write a poem about a handsome man who prolonged the moment before a kiss.

Beba smiled at her and pulled her deeper into the pool. She stopped and pushed him a little harder. He fell backwards into the pool and remained underwater.

Kambi panicked. She waded through the water in search of him. When she found him, she crouched above him and dragged him out of the water.

"Wake up, Beba," she cried, shaking his still body. Pressing her ears to his chest, she listened. His heart was beating. She didn't know much about the heart and its machinations, but she knew a bit about mouth-to-mouth resuscitation. She could hear her heart pounding like a talking drum in her chest. She had read articles on resuscitation techniques. She'd even seen lifeguards in *Baywatch* conduct some. Bending over, Kambi sucked in air and breathed into his mouth. Suddenly, she felt his moist lips parting. His hand held her face, kissed her. She moaned slightly and lifted her face.

He laughed.

"Oh, you'd resurrect any drowned man with those lips of yours," he joked.

Kambi frowned. Her wet shirt and jeans stuck to her skin. She knew Beba wouldn't have to look hard to see through the thin layer of wet clothing.

"That was not funny. You – you are such a clown ... an actor in fact," she stuttered. A treacherous smile tugged at the corners of her lips. "I can't believe you just fooled me." The dimples slowly appeared in her cheeks.

"What?" he said.

Springing up to his feet, he tried in vain to dust the sand off his wet jeans. She started to laugh. He laughed too. Kambi watched his hand quivering as though it itched for something important. She knew he wanted to hold her, to carry her high in the air but was controlling himself.

Kambi paused and added, "I'm surprised at me." She was telling him, and herself too. What a miracle, to be able to laugh from the depths of her heart!

"I'm wondering the same too," he said. "You're different. You came across as ..."

"Uptight?" she said, her eyebrows arched.

"Well," he said, squeezing her hand, "More like stuck-up?"

She frowned.

"Look, if this is about that time in school and the Book Jam—"

"It's not about the Book Jam incident," he assured her. "Sit. And who says a lady can't turn down a man's advances?"

Kambi breathed heavily. They sat back to back on the boulder. Rays of sunlight threw playing patterns on their heads.

"Let's have dinner together," Beba said, rising. Kambi smiled.

"At the Terrace?" she asked.

A soft breeze ruffled the leaves of the trees. Her shoulders quivered.

"Yes," he said, nodding in agreement. "Does 7pm give you enough time to get ready?"

Dinner wouldn't encroach on her work time, she thought. And a girl had to eat dinner. What would it hurt to eat with a man she liked?

Her lips tugged up in a smile as she said, "7pm is fine."

***

They sat in a corner of the restaurant eating their dinner. The restaurant was quiet, not as busy as it had been the day before. Kambi found the jazz music soothing. She tapped her feet to the beat as she enjoyed the pounded yam and vegetable soup. And she could tell Beba liked the meal; his smiling face and smacking lips gave him away.

She couldn't stop thinking about their tour – the horse ride, the visit to the stable, the stolen kisses by the mountain pool – and the way she felt about him.

She took a spoonful of her soup and looked up at him. Their eyes locked.

"What?" she asked, smiling. She could hear her heart pounding louder, faster. What was happening to her? She reached out and grabbed her glass of water, which she drained in one gulp.

Beba laughed and shook his head. "Nothing. Just staring," he said.

He had finished his food by now. He washed his hands with the bowl of water the waiter had left and cocked his head to the left.

Kambi picked at her half-full bowl and sighed.

"Your parents still live in Port Harcourt, right?" he said, smiling.

Kambi nodded. Where was this conversation going, she wondered.

"I hope your parents are well. And your sister? Can't remember her name again," he continued. He'd stopped snapping his fingers. He looked frustrated at his inability to remember her sister's name.

"Dianabasi. But we all call her Diana."

"Yes. Diana!" he said. "How could I forget?"

"My parents are well." Kambi paused and added, "Diana is fine." She refilled her glass with water. Briefly, Kambi thought of Diana and her twin sons. They had exchanged text messages when she'd returned to her room. The twins were ill – why did they always fall ill at the same time? – and Diana was shuttling between her office and the hospital.

Kambi hoped the questions wouldn't probe further. Beba didn't have to know everything. Especially not about the rift she was having with her mother. So she shifted the conversation around.

"Do you have any memories of your birth mother?" He shook his head.

"I have no memories of her. Not sure I know how maternal love feels," he said, pushing his plate aside. "How does it feel?"

Turning her head slightly, she said, "It's nothing too special. Sometimes it can be stifling. Wait a minute ... you never knew your mum at all?"

"Yeah. Apparently, there's a whole lot of history involved and my father has chosen to be quiet about it."

Kambi's jaw dropped. She reached out and rubbed his hand.

"Is she in Europe?" she asked. "Wherever she is, you should at least go and see her. Life is too short."

"That's the problem," he said and sighed. "My father knows her whereabouts but he won't tell me. Except ..."

Kambi dropped her spoon in her bowl and shuddered at the noisy clanging. Why would a father keep mother and child apart? It didn't make sense.

A chubby-faced waitress came to their table. "Have you finished?" she asked. Kambi nodded in agreement. She cleared the plates, smiling politely at Beba. Kambi eyed her, willing her to leave as they both stood up.

"Can we finish this discussion at your chalet?" he asked.

Kambi sighed with relief as she stood up. She slung her bag over her shoulder and they left the restaurant.

Buttoning her jacket, she followed Beba to his sports car. The sky shone with the bright light of the full moon. She sat down, thinking of Beba's predicament. She blocked out the sound of the engine with a replay of his voice. The longing in his voice had made her sad.

The car pulled up at her driveway. She rubbed the back of his hand and stared at him. What was she to say at this point? She willed herself to wait until she'd heard the rest of the story.

"Come inside," she said as she stepped out of the car. She walked to her door and opened it, not even looking back. She slouched into her couch and waited with her arms folded across her chest. She smelled the sweet scent of his cologne mingled with sweat. And she exhaled.

She looked up as he walked towards her and she could see his large eyes glistening with tears.

"I need your help," he said.

"How can I help? What can I do?" She pulled him to the couch, urging him to sit. What was she supposed to say to this grown man who was on the verge of tears? She, who had always considered her own family to be the most dysfunctional in the world?

How could she help? Stage a campaign, or organise a press conference or a peaceful protest? Family matters were never resolved by airing dirty laundry. How could he enlist her help?

He stood up, paced around the living room. Then, he stopped in front of her. Sinking to his knee, he took her hand in his. Kambi's eyebrows rose; Beba stared straight into her eyes.

"Let's get engaged ..."

She shook her head in bewilderment; her lips pressed together and her eyes blinked uncontrollably. "Huh?"

"Or, rather, let's pretend to be engaged. I know, I know. I really, really like you. And I can feel the tension between us. Hell, everyone can see the sparks we emit—"

"Everyone but me. What sparks?" she broke in, wrinkling her nose in mockery. She hadn't bargained for this. Couldn't he tell?

He craned his neck and stared at her. Then, he bit his lips quietly as if considering the possibility that she could be serious.

Placing his hand on her shoulders, he continued, but in a low voice: "My father will see those sparks and believe us. And thankfully, my father is not an ethnic chauvinist

... I am a living testimony. He promised to give me a lead to finding my mother, if, and only if, I brought home a woman to whom I am engaged to be married."

My, oh my, Kambi thought. How scary things had become! She looked at him; the man who broke down her defences, the man who made her poetry a little different, the man who'd rescued her that cold night.

Too much information to process all at once, Kambi thought.

"Wait." Kambi raised her hands, shrugged him off, and said, "What if it all goes wrong?"

"It won't. Please be optimistic." He tried to hold her hand, but she turned her back to him.

She had to be sure exactly what Beba wanted from her. Would his request interfere with her plans? Kambi didn't believe that women ought to abandon their aspirations and values in order to fulfil a man's whims. But what did she have to lose by pretending to be his fiancée?

True, she wanted to help him, but she didn't want a real engagement. It was bad enough that the memories of the failed engagement to Victor were still fresh in her mind.

"But why me? Why not some other girl? Surely you're friendly with other girls," she said.

"I've met other girls, but none are as confident, original, and beautiful as you. I want someone I can trust, not just anyone. This mission is important to me."

"I know, but ..."

"Please give this a chance. You don't have to love. Only

see this as a win-win situation. You get an opportunity to open your heart to something new. It's the easiest way to forget past hurts, to move on. And I'll find my mother." He squeezed her hand lightly.

She saw tears glisten in his eyes. Men ought never to cry, she thought.

Beba continued: "I will respect your decision, if you refuse. But please understand that you're the only person I know who can pull this off, the only person I can trust to keep this between us; I know you won't betray me."

"But my job?" she stuttered. "How long would I have to stay here?"

"Not long. And you'll get twice your salary until you decide to return to your old job. I shall take care of your expenses while you're here playing fiancée," he said. "And you get to keep the engagement ring after everything."

The offer was tempting. She was becoming a paid actress to star in a reality show where she had to pretend to be in love with a handsome man she liked. What would happen to her poetry collection? She'd have to hide the engagement from Tima while she completed her poems.

And did this mean that they would put the attraction between them on the back burner?

"I know you aren't ready for love," he said as though he'd read her thoughts, "so you must trust me to keep my part of the bargain."

It had never been in her character to take leaps in the

dark. But something in her leapt at this offer. She wanted to do something different, to test new waters.

"I'll have to think about it," she said.

"You can think about it," he said.

Kambi slouched in the couch and buried her face in her hands. With only a few poems to go and a series of revisions, she could manage somehow. It couldn't be so bad, living like a princess, pretending to be engaged to a man whom she liked, while running the risk of losing her contract and missing the deadline for the prize.

She walked towards the door and threw it open. A gust of wind hit their faces. "I can't think with you standing here," she said.

Beba sighed and looked at her. "Don't be angry with me. We have a party tomorrow evening."

"I know. But I want to be left alone now," she said, eyeing him.

As soon as he'd walked out of the chalet, she shut the door, and walked to her bedroom.

Nine

The fire glowed steadily. A noisy group of people circled the fire in a feverish dance. Occasionally, some couples danced inside the circle, close to the fire, while others danced outside the circle, beside the bar. In between the bar and the circle, Kambi and Beba jiggled their shoulders and waists to the Naija jamz music that blared from the speakers. It was as though they had never had that discussion. Kambi had prepared for the party as planned. On their way to the bar, Beba had offered a tactful apology for dumping all his mother issues on her.

"You are a good dancer," he shouted above the din of the music. It was the only way they could hear each other.

"Are you mocking me?" she replied, laughing. He shook his head. Then he twirled her around. She giggled.

More people poured in. Screams of excitement floated on the warm night breeze.

"Let's sit down," Kambi said, panting. He nodded.

Beba led the way as they waded through the throngs of people holding frothing glasses of beer, chatting in loud voices and laughing. They brushed past the swaying couples standing in front of the bar.

Having found empty chairs, they moved them around to a slightly secluded spot where they could get a better view of the bonfire, the boisterous guests and the dancing couples.

Beba kept looking over his shoulder. Kambi turned once and saw a tall man smoking by the bar. The man disappeared into the shadows. She clutched Beba's arms and he squeezed her hand. She exhaled.

The music died down. A man cleared his throat. Kambi looked up. Bem was wielding the microphone. She smiled and waved. *Am I ready to be called upon?* she wondered. Reaching into her pocket for her poem, she bit her lower lip. The poem wasn't there. She turned to Beba.

"It's our turn to perform!" Beba said, cheering.

Kambi stood up, masking her frustration with a forced smile. *What will I do, now that I don't have the poem?*

There was a round of applause as Beba led her upstage.

Bending over the microphone, she smiled. "Hello everyone," she said, looking sideways and watching as Beba slung an electric guitar across his chest.

Different responses came in: catcalls, cheers and more rounds of applause.

She looked at Beba and felt a poem pouring through her being.

"I shall recite a very short poem titled 'Someday'. I hope you enjoy it."

Beba strummed the guitar with dexterous fingers. Kambi closed her eyes, replayed the kiss at the grotto.

Someday is a day yet to become
And yet everyday, someday comes
Its presence so familiarly unfamiliar

We, unknowingly, expect its perfect replica
Seeming much more promising that we
procrastinate

Tomorrow, a precious moment in time,
Which recedes like the rainbow on earth's horizon
But hangs around like a friendly ghost
Its advent announced by midnight's chime
Its ardent and only holy host

The future sits on fate's palm
Stretching our hopes limitlessly
For someday is the day our dreams come true
But someday is only fair to the faithful
Everyday is a blessing, and so is someday.

A round of applause filled the air. Beba held Kambi's hand, and they both bowed. There were more screams of 'hear, hear!' as they walked back to their seats.

At their seats, admirers shook their hands, congratulating them. The bonfire party had continued with a highlife band presentation. Beba cocked his head and raised his bushy eyebrows. Kambi returned his stare, shrugged her shoulders.

"You are a natural poet, you know?" Beba said.

"And you're a grand guitarist," she replied, smiling.

"Me? I just play in my bedroom, when I am alone. It's therapeutic," he said, squeezing her hand.

She felt strange stirrings in her heart; electrifying shivers shot through her being. If I was his guitar, she wondered, how wonderful it would feel to be strummed by his fingers ...

"Want something to drink? Wine or beer or malt?" Beba asked.

Two lines appeared on her forehead as she considered the options.

"Malt," she said. Her voice was firm.

Beba pushed his seat back and strode to the bar. Kambi heard someone hail him "Oyinbo, how far?"

And Beba replied, "Fine. And you?"

Hands clapped in a manly handshake.

Kambi watched the bright-yellow fire glow in the night. Smoke drifted up into the sky, and ashes spiralled and whirred in a rough circle before floating wherever the wind blew. She imagined that her life drifted like the smoke and ashes. Tima had asked for the first ten pages, and Kambi had sent them.

Someone shoved a frothing glass of beer under her lips. The stench of beer hit her nose. Startled at the intrusion, she looked at the man with disdain.

"Cut my spit!" the burly man cried.

Kambi jerked back and reached for her pepper spray on impulse. Then she stopped herself.

"No!" she snapped, frowning at him. She scanned the crowd, searching for Beba. He was nowhere in sight.

"Cut my spit!" the man sang.

Kambi slapped his hand away. Some of his beer spilled on the floor. She eyed his chubby cheeks, his round shiny head, and his small hands. He was a short man, but he spoke with a shocking confidence that forced Kambi to dislike him from the moment he had appeared with his weird proposal.

"Leave me alone," Kambi said. "I don't know what you're asking." Waving him away dismissively, she looked around for Beba.

"You're a visitor? Oyinbo Beba's girl?"

"Beba's friend. Yes," she said, stressing the word 'friend'. It was annoying, having to sit by the light of a bonfire and explain her relationship with Beba. What were they now? Friends or a sham couple with motives? And, now that they had kissed, were they romantically involved? Now that they were stuck at that precarious point between being friends with benefits and announcing an engagement, what were they?

"Utibe," said the intruder, as he extended his hand. "My name is Utibe."

"Kambi," she replied, without accepting his handshake.

With slurred words, he launched into a discourse about Beba. Kambi tuned him out. She finally spotted Beba clutching two cans in each hand and standing by the bar talking to a red-haired mixed-race girl.

She is quite tall ... and look at those long legs, Kambi thought. She subdued the urge to feel jealous or panicked. "Jealousy is a petty emotion. And I am beyond jealousy," Kambi muttered under her breath.

But have I set myself up for heartbreak?

Kambi looked up at Beba wondering why the red-haired girl was patting him in such a familiar way on the arm. Why was she pulling him to the dance floor? Kambi's jaw dropped in shock, which soon turned to relief as Beba shrugged off the woman's hand. At that moment, Beba locked eyes with Kambi.

Kambi looked up and registered that Utibe was no longer asking her to 'cut his spit', but was saying: "Beba is a nice guy. Has a degree in metallurgical engineering. Spent one year as a Peace Corps volunteer in Liberia. Did you know that? And he has a Master's degree. Did you know? And the mining company here ... You see, he wants to further develop the community ..."

Kambi nodded. She needed to get some air. Why was she feeling uneasy?

"So, cut my spit," said Utibe, in a more friendly tone.

The music changed and everyone screamed, "Yay!"

"UT, you're harassing my friend," Beba said, shoving Utibe with his shoulder. Kambi sighed in relief. What had taken Beba so long?

Utibe turned. Beba had a can of drink in each hand – a can of Smirnoff Ice and a can of malt.

"I'm sorry," Utibe said.

Beba handed Kambi the can of malt and a plastic straw. "Utibe works for my cousin in the bar and resturant," he said.

Kambi nodded and frowned. "Really?" she said. She

asked him if she could have a sip of his Smirnoff Ice.

A woman appeared and threaded her hands around Utibe's bulging stomach. Kambi recognised her as the receptionist at the resort. "Mina?" Kambi asked, turning to Beba. "Your sister."

"You've already met?" Beba asked, frowning.

Kambi nodded.

"I see fate already brought you two together," Mina said. "I'll just take my man away," she added, as she nibbled Utibe's ear. The man chuckled and staggered. "He's drunk," Mina mouthed, steadying Utibe as she led him to a seat by the bonfire.

Beba looked at Kambi. "Are you alright? He didn't mean any harm, poor guy," Beba said.

"Poor Mina, you mean?"

"Mina's love is tough enough. Anyway, it is a sign of courteousness to offer strangers your cup of beer," Beba said. He was holding Kambi's hand.

They sat in their cane chairs, sipping their drinks and watching the bonfire. The fire was very different from the restaurant's decorative glow. The fire here flared and burned skywards, emitting enough heat to warm everyone.

"Just curious," she started, "the red-haired girl ..."

Kambi wondered if she had any right to feel possesive about Beba.

"Oh, Bernice? She's a correspondent and travel writer. Why?" Beba said, smiling.

"Like I said, I was just curious," Kambi said, shrugging indifferently. "Just saw you two chatting like old friends. That's all."

Beba laughed. "Bernice is not a threat at all. We had a very brief relationship, which was a bad idea. But we're still friends." Beba looked back again.

"Oh good," Kambi replied. Worry lines appeared on her forehead and she downed his can of Smirnoff.

She began to read signs into the way the smoke circled and drifted sideways. She thought about the things he'd said at the pool. She remembered the look in his eyes. Every fibre of her being wanted to be a part of his quest. Not just because he had been a wonderful friend so far, but because she really cared about him.

Turning to Beba, she imagined being fleetingly engaged to him, standing by him. She had thought up strategies to protect herself, to ensure she wouldn't be taken advantage of.

She would rather walk away and focus on her project. It'd be difficult, but she'd have nipped a potentially bad situation in the bud.

Kambi sipped her drink and faced Beba. Her head swirled. The shadows of the crowed soared into the sky by the fire.

Lifting her hands in the air, Kambi said, "Dance with me. Imagine that this is our last night together." She took his hand and twirled round.

She turned her back to him and began to do the

seductive Konko Below dance. When she faced Beba, she was a different girl. She maintained eye contact with him. They swayed to the rhythm. Beba moonwalked round her, and she squealed with delight. Throwing her head back, she laughed.

***

Beba admired the way Kambi danced with abandon. He liked the way she swung her arms and wriggled low as though they were both in a world of their own.

The live band started a highlife song. Kambi wrapped her hands around his neck and swayed. A smile played on her lips. Beba held her waist and breathed in her ear: "Marry me," he said.

Kambi chuckled. "Don't joke about things like this at a bonfire party. You might regret it," she said. A whiff of alcohol hit his nostrils. He swallowed hard, and bit his lips.

Smiling rather coyly, he winked at her as though his eyes were saying, 'We're in cahoots, remember?'

But when he opened his mouth, he said: "Let's make this engagement official."

His voice had risen a notch so that people standing two metres from them turned and stared. He dropped on one knee, opened a small white box with an engagement ring inside.

Her hand flew to her chest. "Oh my," she gasped, "it's so beautiful."

Beba took the hand she'd held out and slid the ring onto the ring finger. There was a round of applause as he carried her and twirled her around.

Ten

She tried recalling the events of the previous night – the bonfire, the red-haired girl, the dances and the proposal. In the morning light, the ring gleamed. She considered the decision, and wondered how it could affect the course of her life. What effect might this have on her project, she wondered.

The jarring ring of her phone jerked her out of her thoughts. She clicked the receiver button.

"Good morning, Tima," Kambi said, with a loud yawn. "I've sent the first batch of poems. Did ..."

"Yes, I got your e-mail. But what's this news I'm hearing about you being engaged?"

Kambi stuttered, ran her fingers through her locks of hair. *Why am I wearing his shirt?*

"Who told you I was engaged?"

Oh shit! And I am lying in his bed. But where is he? I've been so high!

"I know people who live and work at Obudu. It's a small town. Word spreads fast, Kambi."

"Oh."

"Surely this wasn't part of the plan," she muttered as she checked herself. Bra still hooked. Check. Panties still on. Check. But could she be sure?

"Oh? Should I regard the news as fact or fiction?"

"People talk too much," Kambi said. A heavy silence

hung like the morning fog between them. Tima would be disappointed if she told her the truth. Out of obligation, she added, "Don't believe everything you hear."

Kambi heard Tima heave a sigh of relief.

"You mustn't forget the deadline for the prize," she said. "You'll have to send them at the end of each day. I think you should stop seeing that guy. He's a distraction."

"But my writing has changed a bit since I met him. You said so yourself."

"I did? Was I exaggerating? Perhaps. But this project has to be given priority over everything else. Period!"

Kambi pulled at her hair. She wanted to scream insults into the phone. But then she saw Beba and her jaw dropped. Tray in hand, he was walking into the room, grinning.

Putting her index finger across her lips, Kambi urged him to be quiet. She nodded into the phone and said, "Noted. I shall send them as you have requested." The line went dead.

"Morning, Candy," Beba said, setting down the tray he was carrying.

So he has returned to calling me Candy. Why is he glowing?

"Good morning, Bee," Kambi said, smiling. "You're wearing an apron?"

"I made us breakfast," he said, gesturing to the tray of tea, sardines, eggs, oats and toast.

He shouldn't have bothered. But how sweet of him

to have made me breakfast. Victor could never make breakfast; only trouble.

Rich as Beba was, Kambi knew that he could easily have got his chef to do the cooking and serving. Or he could have ordered a takeaway from Terrace. Clearly, he was trying to make an impression.

Staring at him intently, she thanked him. "What happened last night?" Worry lines appeared on her forehead as she quizzed him.

I remember the dance, the drop-dead gorgeous red-haired ex-girlfriend, and, vaguely, the ring; but nothing about how I got into your shirt and your bed.

"Last night was beautiful and ... eventful," he crooned, pouring hot milk from the jug.

Then he said, "You capped it by vomiting all over your clothes. They're in the washing machine right now." He pointed to the jar of white cubes. "Sugar?" he asked and she shook her head. "I had to bring you here so that I could monitor you all through the night. And I wanted a chance to actually bring you breakfast in bed. Don't worry about your rules. I will never violate a single one of them. You kept muttering them in your sleep."

She sipped her glass of warm milk and smiled. "A girl has got to look out for herself. These principles or rules, as you call them, are supposed to help protect my dignity. You men are predators, hunters ..."

"I'm not trying to hunt you, am I?"

"Who knows?"

Kambi stared at Beba's smiling face. He ran his fingers through his hair.

What woman in her right mind would stop seeing such a wonderful man because her bossy agent wants her to complete a project, Kambi wondered. She could feel the tension between them as they looked into each other's eyes.

"So we have to take you shopping. My father loves clothes made from print material," he said.

Kambi stared at him; her eyes widened and her head tilted to one side. "Print wax? Like Ankara?"

"Yes," Beba said.

Kambi wanted to protest, but she had come this far and agreed to help him. She would have loved to wear her own clothes, but she didn't have any outfits made of African print wax.

Whenever she saw Kaycee's Woodin and Vlisco designs, she was awestruck by their sheer beauty. Yet she never found the time to shop for the materials and send them to the tailor. Beba's words broke her train of thought.

"... The driver will take us to Tinapa to buy print cloths," he said. "Then, a tailor in Calabar will sew them as soon as possible. We have only a few days."

"My old friend Kaycee lives in Calabar. She makes lovely clothes. We could check out her designs online. I'd like her to make the clothes," Kambi said, reaching for her handbag, which was lying across the room. She whipped out the small notepad and pen she always carried around. She tore out a page and wrote down Kaycee's website address.

"Kaycee's fashion website," she said, as she handed the paper to Beba. Standing up, she breathed out deeply. He ironed her half-dry clothes while she cleared away their breakfast table.

He dropped her off at her chalet.

***

Back in her room, she felt unfathomably light-hearted, but she didn't rationalise it too much. She unpacked her handbag and found six missed calls on her phone – all from Diana. She wondered why she hadn't heard the phone ringing in her bag. Kambi hadn't spoken to her sister in a while, but she couldn't return her calls just yet. She wasn't in the mood for a long conversation, so she sent a text message and switched off the phone.

She spent most of the day writing long poems. She didn't notice the hours passing.

During brief breaks, she uploaded short prose poems not meant for the collection onto her blog – poems about the bonfire party and the engagement proposal. The characters were fictional and quite enigmatic. She didn't want to reveal crucial details of the plan. While she would have liked to tell it all to her readers, she didn't want to be judged for her unconventional ways.

Who knew what harm it could do to Beba's chances of finding his mother?

The sun was high up in the sky when Kambi and Beba arrived in Tinapa to select suitable print wax materials. After an hour of arguing on which they should buy, Kambi phoned Kaycee. But, by the time Kaycee arrived, Beba had paid for five different patterns, and so they continued their arguments at her fashion studio in Calabar town.

Kambi was enjoying every part of their bickering. She found that she was drawn to men who encouraged her openness; men who allowed her to express herself. Talking to Beba was even more exciting because he was a good listener. And when he fought, he fought fair; he never resorted to name-calling.

But Kaycee didn't impose her ideas on them. She was adept in marketing her designs and services. Having ensured her guests were comfortably seated, she allowed them to talk about their expectations. Occasionally, she intervened and suggested the most suitable designs for Kambi's figure. Kambi was impressed by her friend's business skills.

At 28, Kaycee ran her own fashion business. And, in spite of all the stiff competition, she still managed to do well.

"I'm proud of your accomplishments," said Kambi. They both laughed.

Kaycee couldn't give her a high five, because she didn't want to disturb the apprentice who was taking Kambi's measurements. Instead, they made small talk. Kaycee oohed and aahed at the beauty of the engagement ring.

"You're really engaged to that gorgeous man? How come?" Kaycee whispered, cupping her chubby face in her palms. Her fair-complexioned face contrasted with Kambi's dark-brown skin.

"I heard he has an interesting track record. I heard ..." Kaycee said.

"You're always hearing rumours. I like him. Keep your rumours to yourself," Kambi replied, smiling politely.

"What has Diana said about it?" Kaycee asked.

"I haven't told her yet. It isn't what you think. Please keep it to yourself," Kambi said. She knew Kaycee's strengths, but keeping secrets wasn't one of them.

"I don't understand you," she replied. "But he looks ..." Kambi tuned her out. Briefly, she craned her neck.

Beba was standing outside the shop, speaking into his phone.

The apprentice got all the measurements. Kayccc showed Kambi and Beba the design they had agreed on.

"But I could change it slightly, if I think up a better design," Kaycee said as she wrote down the prices.

Beba collected the bill. And Kaycee promised that the outfits would be ready in a matter of days.

Before they left Calabar for the mountain resort, Kaycee whispered into Kambi's ear, "Better hold on to this one." She gestured towards Beba with her nose. "Hold on – either by hook or by crook."

Kambi laughed. It was the kind of thing Diana would

have said. "I thought you said he was a philanderer," said Kambi.

"Having observed him for a few hours, I'd say he's not as bad as I heard he was. And he seems to adore you. Just feels right, that's all."

Kambi laughed and climbed into the car.

Eleven

"Mind your step. I don't want you to fall off this canopy walkway," Beba said.

Kambi gasped, breathing in the warm earthy air. She was amazed at its freshness since little sunlight managed to penetrate through the trees and shrubs.

She didn't want to imagine falling 20 feet off the canopy walkway into the marshy forest floor. Her grip on the ropes tightened as she said, "I can't fall off this thing. The holes are small."

Chuckling, Beba shook the rope. The walkway swayed. Kambi squealed, placed one hand on her chest, and glared at him.

"You do realise that we'll both fall about 20 feet down, don't you?" she said.

"I know."

She listened to the chirruping birds, the chirping crickets. A porcupine scurried into a hole in the ground. Touring the Beecheve rainforest had been more exciting than she had expected it to be.

She'd phoned her agent and apologised. They'd agreed that Kambi would focus on completing the project.

Now, walking through the warm forest, she wondered if she was doing the right thing. She felt as though her survival depended on the completion of the manuscript.

She needed to prove that she wasn't a failure. Her family

would be proud and happy. Everyone would forget about the botched wedding and focus on the new book. At least that was how she'd planned it. But the stunning ring on her finger was doing nothing to help her.

She stopped moving. She considered throwing the ring in his face and running back to her room. But she was torn between her feelings for him and the quest to complete her collection of poems. A part of her wanted to be there for him and help him find his mother. She loved basking in the attention he was giving her, but she couldn't risk failing at this task, not after everything she'd put into it. Her reputation was at stake.

She felt his hand on her shoulder, and turned. "Are you alright?" he asked.

She saw the concern in his eyes and felt her resolve melting.

Willing herself to be strong, she exhaled and said, "I'm fine." She flashed a wide smile.

"Are you sure?"

She nodded and bit her lips. "Of course. I'm fine," she said. Her voice was stern as she carried on walking. She cajoled herself into enjoying the trip. Who said she couldn't get inspiration from this tour?

She focused on the giant trees. They stood sturdy and tall. Branches of kapok and acacia trees intertwined like lovers.

"Did you come here often as a child?" Kambi asked.

"Yes," Beba said. "Back then, there were a lot of

birds, insects and lizards. Once, we saw a two-horned chameleon. We were so scared, we ran away."

Kambi chuckled. "But you returned shortly afterwards," she said matter-of-factly.

"Of course. We were curious children. Once, we saw a leopard running off with a porcupine. Just once, though. We didn't see many wild cats, but there were a lot of stories about their exploits."

Beba held her right hand as they approached the end of the walkway.

She reached out for some asara fruits hanging from a low branch. Her leg slipped, and she lost her balance and fell into Beba's arms.

"Careful," he said, helping her up.

She thanked him and reached out again. This time, she plucked the tomato-shaped, tough-skinned fruit.

"Are these edible?" she asked, showing him the wet fruits.

"Not sure. But my uncle used to bag and export the fruit. I heard its oils are valuable."

Kambi nodded. She tried to reach out for some wet leaves from an acacia tree but changed her mind.

They sat in the metal tree house and talked. Beba held her hand and told her that he'd visited his father earlier that day. Kambi listened as they watched rodents scurrying in and out of holes, mating larks and hunting lizards. Just as Kambi began to relax, it started to rain. They hurried back to the ranch, out of the rainforest.

They jogged until the rain subsided. Panting, they sat on a felled fig tree. Kambi plucked orchids and ferns off the tree bark.

"I had a nice time today," Beba said, taking her hand.

Raising her chin, she stared into his face. He was smiling shyly and beaming with a charming boyishness that excited her. She squeezed his hand.

The raw drizzling rain drove them further up the hill. They ran in the direction of her chalet. Kambi's heart beat faster as they rushed into the chalet and shut the door. Overwhelmed by passion, they smothered each other with kisses.

Beba led her to the sofa, watching her as she lay with her eyes closed. He kissed the nape of her neck, and paused to look at her face. Kambi opened her eyes and smiled at him. Her hand traced the line on his long pointed nose. He sighed and pressed his lips to hers. Lying on her back, he kissed her upper lip, and then caressed her back. He took her lower lip and teased. Kambi wrapped her legs around his waist.

They moaned in unison as his mouth covered hers. Slowly, he slipped his hand between her thighs. She sighed, tightened her arms round his neck. His hands caressed, slowly creeping up her waist. He paused, and circled his thumb around her bellybutton. Kambi leaned over, flicking her tongue in his right ear, then nibbled on his earlobe. Beba groaned and hugged her tightly. He didn't want the moment to end.

She felt him wanting to melt into her.

Stop! Stop! Stop!

Heeding the voice of reason, she pushed him away, caught her breath and said, "Hold on." She gasped again, as he kissed her on her neck. "Hold on," she whispered, pulling away slowly.

Beba sighed.

"Forgive me," he said. She faced him.

"For what?"

"Rushing you," he said, running his finger through his wet hair. "I find you irresistible. Sometimes, I see your face in my sleep. You're always on ..."

She held up her hand and said, "I take some responsibility for getting carried away. Everything is happening too fast. We should slow down, you know." Kambi pursed her lips, wondering why she was imploring him to place reason over passion. Her body was still on fire. Oh, she wanted him to kiss and hold her.

"Yes. We should," he said, biting his lips.

Kambi turned her face. She was so smitten with his charm; she knew her eyes would betray her emotions. Why did her heart leap in excitement whenever he was around? Why was she fascinated by his nobleness and calmness? How many men could control their urges and respect a woman half as much? Not many.

"I informed my father of our engagement," he said.

"When?"

"This morning. I wanted to let him know before the rumour-mongers reached him."

Kambi nodded.

It would be over soon, and she would return to the life she had known before her holiday.

***

Beba was thinking about the visit to his father.

He'd guessed that his father must have heard gossip. His father lived in an exotic mansion in the town. The town was so small that word spread fast. When his father set eyes on him, he said, "I heard the news today. Congratulations on your engagement. Bring her home to see your old man."

Beba had gone home thinking of the best way to break the news to Kambi. But, watching her from the corner of his eye, he could see that she was breathing heavily, her chest rising and falling in rhythm.

He gave her shoulder a reassuring squeeze. Tension crackled in the air between them.

"He is looking forward to meeting you," Beba added.

Kambi turned to him and nodded. She took a bottle of water from the fridge and drank. Then she sighed and said, "It's OK. I'm ready."

Beba smiled and nodded. He respected her for her courage.

He took his jacket off the hook and pecked her on the cheek. "Goodnight," he said. Standing in the doorway, he studied her expression.

"Goodnight," she replied. Then she shut the door.

Beba walked away. *The Retired General will have no choice but to accept you as a worthy bride-to-be.*

Twelve

On the designated date, Beba squeezed Kambi's hand as they stood in front of the imposing door, waiting to be ushered in.

It was a moonless night and a strong wind howled. Kambi didn't know what to expect. But she was excited about the uncertainty of the outcome. She had almost completed the poetry collection. The last poem was supposed to be a rhapsody about Beba's search for his mother. She was hoping for the best.

Suddenly, the door opened.

"Welcome, Kambi and Beba," said the butler, bowing slightly. He stood aside, holding the door open.

Kambi's hand flew to her chest in surprise. *The butler knows my name.*

"Mr Steve," Beba said. "How do you do?"

His hand curved round her waist, guiding her into the mansion. Together, they marched along the wide corridors, lined with thick rugs.

Kambi walked gingerly, throwing cursory glances at the paintings and sculptures that hung from the walls.

His parents have good taste in art.

Feeling pleased, she looked at her Vlisco wrapper-styled gown, wondering if her attire was suitable for the dinner.

They stopped at the end of the corridor and walked down a couple of low stairs, into a sparsely furnished living room. Seated on the leather couch were his father and stepmother. Kambi curtseyed as she guessed tradition would demand. Was she overdoing it? After all, she was only an acting fiancée.

"Welcome, you must be Kambi," the old man said in his baritone voice. He rose and held out his hand.

Beba started to speak but the man broke in: "Retired General Gabriel Beba Sambe," he said, shaking Kambi's hand. "And this is Lady Eunice Sambe, my wife."

Kambi shook their hands and smiled. There seemed to be a high wall between Beba and his father. *Men and their bloated egos*. Kambi stared at Beba from the corner of her eye, willing him to break the ice. Beba cleared his throat and smiled. The imaginary barrier crumbled, and Beba saluted – half-jocularly, half-robotically. His father reciprocated. The men laughed and hugged.

"Beba, good to see you again," the retired general said. "I've been waiting for this moment to come."

Kambi smiled, tactfully. She pressed her lips together and turned away. She'd thought about this decision, had always felt right about playing this role and returning to her life when it was over. She owed him this small favour for protecting her in the past.

"Let's sit," Beba's stepmother said. Her voice was thin and laced with a lilt that Kambi found unique, musical and interesting. Threading her long hands through the men's arms, Eunice led them to the dining table.

"Dinner is getting cold," she added.

The men didn't argue. They settled at the dining table,

where Eunice began to uncover the dishes, until all the delicacies were on display. Kambi admired Eunice's style. She seemed to be adept at handling her men.

The butler arrived with a tray of wine glasses and poured the wine. They sipped in the fragile silence of the room. They exchanged glances as they drank until Eunice broke the silence with a cry.

"Oh, for God's sake, this is an announcing-the-engagement party not a funeral. Let's eat!"

She ladled spoonfuls of tomato stew and rice onto the china plates. Kambi passed the plates around.

"So, you're a poet?" Beba's father asked.

"Yes. I write and perform poetry in my spare time. It's a means of catharsis much like Beba's guitar playing," Kambi replied.

"You write poems? That's wonderful," Eunice pitched in. "But aren't you scared sometimes? Of failure? Of rejection? That you'll die a miserable pauper?" She dropped her fork, clasped her fingers and watched Kambi.

"I used to occasionally slip into depression," Kambi said, lifting her chin, "until I realised that fear and sadness did nothing but eat at my heart and soul. Now, I write not for the fortune or the fame but because I find fulfilment in it. Really not for anything else. One day at a time." She paused, and then added, "But I have a regular job. I am a broadcaster."

"Is this your first time on the Obudu plateau?" Beba's father asked.

Kambi swallowed and nodded. "Yes, it is."

"Do you like it here?"

"Yes, I do. It must be a lovely place to live. I love it for its tranquillity and its landmarks." She clenched her fist under the table. She was beginning to feel uncomfortable with her role. Were they impressed, she wondered.

"How long have you and Beba known each other?" Beba's father asked. He chewed his rice slowly as he peered at Kambi in anticipation of an answer. His face radiated under the glare of the chandelier, and his jaw tightened, finely chiselled like Beba's.

"Six years!"

"Four years!"

Beba and Kambi turned to each other and looked away just as quickly. Why hadn't they discussed that part?

The retired general dropped his fork and stared at the couple.

"Is this some kind of joke?" he said.

"No, sir," Beba replied in a tone with which one reasonable man may address another.

"He started counting from the first time he saw me at a spoken-word poetry session," Kambi said, "while I counted from our next face-to-face meeting at the Garden City Literary Festival."

The retired general stared silently Kambi and wiped his creased brow with the back of his hand. The tick-tick-tick of the large wall clock made the silence even eerier. Then, he resumed chewing his rice very thoroughly as if on a mission to grind every grain before swallowing.

"Do you love her, Beba?" Eunice asked, quietly. The young couple flushed with embarrassment.

"It's a serious question," she pressed.

Beba stared from Eunice to the retired general to Kambi.

Kambi's heart fluttered in her chest. What if he could see it was all a sham, she wondered. Would it hurt? She shut her eyes and imagined writing a mournful poem when it had all ended.

"Kambi makes my heart beat fast like a konga drum," he said, squinting. "That's love, isn't it?"

Kambi thought about it. What was love?

"Aw, that's good to hear," Eunice said to no-one in particular.

Kambi drank some water and stared at Beba. What would happen next? she wondered. She turned and saw Eunice smiling at her.

"Where do your parents live?" Eunice asked.

"Port Harcourt," Kambi said.

"What do they do?"

"My mother is a nurse and my father a musician."

Eunice nodded. She raised a glass of water to her lips and drank. Kambi threw a glance at Beba. He smiled at her. She looked away.

"Do you have siblings?" Eunice continued.

Kambi nodded. "Just one sister," she said.

"But are you making any plans, yet?"

Smiling excitedly, she searched their faces. Finally, she gestured to Kambi with her glass of wine.

Kambi looked away.

"Ma, please," Beba said, "slow down." He frowned.

Eunice raised her hand in a hushing gesture. "Wait," she said to Beba. "It's the bride's prerogative." Turning to Kambi, she added, "Have you picked a date?"

Kambi shook her head in confusion.

"Er, we are still planning. I have trips to make, Kambi has her job," Beba broke in. Kambi coughed.

The retired general wiped his mouth with a napkin, and touched the back of his son's hand. His face softened as he lifted his glass of wine to his lips. And Kambi realised there was a strong chance that Beba would age to be ruggedly handsome, like his father.

"I guess I have to keep my own end of the bargain," said the retired general. Everyone stared at him.

Silence hung heavily in the air. None of them moved their hands or their lips. Kambi was afraid. She felt sorry for Beba. Looking at him, she felt his heart's palpitations, felt his yearning for love, for acceptance. He was rich and handsome, but there was a void. And she knew it.

One of the maids walked in. Eunice's manicured hands waved the maidservant away with the ease of one used to dismissing people. Her chair scraped the floor as she stood and began gathering the dishes and cutlery.

"Kambi, let's leave the men alone, shall we?" Eunice said, batting her fake eyelashes. With a swift swing of her head, she lifted her chin and gestured towards the door. Kambi grabbed some plates and followed the slap-slap-slap of Eunice's footfalls.

They entered a large, well-lit kitchen. Eunice deposited the plates in the sink and sat on a high stool.

Kambi put down her plates and opened the tap.

"Don't bother with the plates," Eunice said. She was watching her from the corner of her eyes.

Kambi retreated and sat on a stool opposite her. In the bright kitchen lights, Kambi admired Eunice's face – the high cheekbones, the smooth forehead, and the taut skin untouched by age. Her dark-complexioned skin glowed like polished teak.

Mina got her looks from her mother. But how old can she be? She looks no more than 40.

"Your gown is lovely." Eunice said, with an emphasis on the word 'lovely'. "Vlisco, is it?"

Kambi nodded and thanked her for the compliment. "My friend designed and made the dress. She's really good at it. I can give you her number if you want."

"That will be wonderful. Please write it down for me," Eunice said.

Kambi gave her Kaycee's business card. It was the only one she had left, but she could always get another. The older woman thanked her.

"Beba and his father haven't spoken in six years – well, six years before you came along," Eunice said.

"Did he tell you that?"

Kambi shook her head.

"They have been sad men since the last time they quarrelled. That was when Beba left the Peace Corps in Liberia and started making preparations to study for a masters degree in Europe. We didn't even know when he left. You can imagine our relief when he returned to Nigeria to start the mining business," Eunice said, smiling.

Kambi watched her in admiration. There was something unique about her parenting style. Though Kambi tried to wrap her mind around it, she couldn't tell what exactly it was but she knew that Eunice was a good mother.

The men's low-toned discussions droned in the distance.

"Kambi, I have never seen Beba this calm; never seen him this happy," Eunice said.

Kambi cleared her throat. Then she said, "Perhaps it's because he's older now, and richer too." Her voice was low, almost a whisper.

"Perhaps," Eunice said, "but money isn't everything. You see, I have never seen him this content. Not even when he made his first million. He was 26 at the time."

"Really?" Kambi said, leaning her elbow on the white kitchen slab.

"Yes. Believe me," Eunice said. "So tell me, how did you know he was the one?"

Kambi shrugged. I don't know that he is the one, she wanted to say. But that could have whipped up doubts and she didn't want that. So Kambi closed her eyes and searched her soul. Suddenly, a flood of memories came to her mind – the way he'd fought off the attackers, the way he'd shown up at Terrace restaurant, his bright smile, his hands holding her gently ...

"He's smart, fun to be with and easy to talk to," Kambi said with a smile. "He understands me so much it amazes me."

Eunice nodded and waved her slender fingers gently, urging Kambi to continue.

Kambi sat there, reliving the kiss at the grotto, in her chalet, in his apartment. A slight shiver whizzed down her spine.

"When he kisses me, my spirit soars, my heart waltzes in my chest and my breathing pauses. I become a goddess." She stopped, opened her eyes. Was she being too open about her emotions, she wondered. She searched Eunice's face for a hint of disapproval.

"I liked that, Kambi. It sounded like a poem." Eunice said,

Of course, this will all be written down. Finishing my poetry collection was one of the reasons I agreed to play pretend fiancée.

"When I married my husband," Eunice said, looking at Kambi with bright, animated eyes, "I wasn't sure he was the one."

Surprised by Eunice's frankness, Kambi switched to journalist mode.

"So why did you marry him?" Kambi was grateful to turn the searchlights on the other woman.

"Oh well, it was complicated. He was a warlord. I

wanted security. He was kind and generous – he hasn't changed even now. I was quite a wild 18 year-old," she said, giggling.

Kambi imagined a teenage Eunice, at a party flailing her hands over her head and twirling in a heated dance to a highlife song.

"How did that work out?"

"Fine. I am happy with my much older husband, contrary to what everyone expected. We love and respect each other."

Kambi nodded.

Sounds of laughter wafted into the kitchen.

Kambi heard Beba's voice rising above his father's, and she wondered just what the end might be. But did she want it to end?

"Let's check on the men," Eunice said as she alighted from the high stool. Together, they strode into the large living room. The men turned.

"You look like mother and daughter already," the retired general said. His face beamed with joy.

"Kambi's probably the daughter God forgot to give me after Mina arrived."

They laughed.

"We should be on our way," Beba said, picking up a dusty gold box.

Eunice and the General walked with them to where the car was parked. The night was cold. Kambi got into the car thinking back to her first night on the plateau. The car roared and she heard the older couple say their goodbyes.

Kambi looked over her bare shoulders and waved.

Beba waved with one hand and manoeuvred the steering wheel with the other.

Kambi sighed. Raising her chin, she savoured the night sky. It was inky black with a glowing full moon and a sprinkle of twinkling stars. A beautiful night with Beba, she thought.

"Thank you," Beba said, reaching out to her. His soft hands rubbed her thigh.

She gasped.

"For what?" she said.

Briefly, he looked at her and smiled. "You don't know how much you've done for me ..." he sighed and changed gears. After a few minutes, the car pulled over at her chalet. They got out and ambled along the path in silence.

"I had a nice time." Kambi broke the silence. "I like Eunice. What kind of stepmum was she? During your childhood, I mean?"

"I don't know. I was too indifferent a stepchild to let any woman worm her way into my heart."

"That explains a few things," Kambi said. "So did you find out what you need to know about your mother?"

"I got everything. Apparently, my mother is at the tail end of the continent. She lives – or, at least, she used to when my father last had contact with her – in Johannesburg," Beba said, holding her hand. "My father even gave me some pictures of them together," Beba tugged at an envelope in his jacket pocket. They were standing in front of the door now.

"Glad to hear you sounding so excited and optimistic," she said, trying to sound pleased for him. Then she paused and thought about it. She realised she wasn't as excited as she had thought she would be. She didn't want to ask to see the pictures. "So, when do you leave?" she asked, looking down at the doormat. It was becoming more difficult to look at him during what seemed like an informal, but final, goodbye.

"At the weekend. I'll leave for Lagos on Friday, and catch a plane to South Africa on Saturday."

"I guess my work here is done," she said. Her voice was low. She wanted to ask him more: if this was going to be their last goodbye. But it was pointless. Their agreement hadn't included a long-term commitment. She wasn't even sure what she wanted at this point. It hurt to say goodbye.

"I enjoyed every moment we spent together," he said, squeezing her hand.

"I'll leave the resort tomorrow morning," she said. "I start work on Tuesday morning."

She fought back the tears welling up in her eyes. Why was saying goodbye suddenly painful? She shouldn't have started it in the first place. Her hands shivered as she fumbled with her keys. He took them from her.

"No," she said. Her voice was angry. "Don't ... stop being so nice." Snatching the keys from him, she exhaled and unlocked the door.

"I am sorry. I'll do my very best to keep in touch. But I'm really grateful for everything," he said as she crossed the threshold.

Just thank you? Not even a kiss? Her heart cringed. What had happened to her resolve not to fall in love? She used to boast that she never fell in love. Iron lady that she was, she stepped gingerly in and out of love with steady legs. Why were her legs shaking?

Kambi, you have to be the strong independent woman that you have always been.

"Goodbye, Beba," she said with forced courage. Where had that come from?

"Goodbye," he said. Reaching out, he held her face close, brushed his lips against hers. The lingering brush of lips was so tantalising it drove Kambi crazy. Why was he torturing her? She parted her lips and covered his with overwhelming passion. He responded with a matching burst of passion – kiss for kiss, caress for caress.

With one swift movement, he lifted her up, gently carried her into the chalet and shut the door. He placed her on the sofa and dropped conciliatory kisses on the tip of her nose, on her forehead, on her cheeks and chin. Moaning, she cupped his face in her hands and kissed his lower lip. Words were so superfluous that kisses continued the communication of their passions and desires.

As the tempo rose higher, her knees grew weaker, as did her resolve. *Careful Kambi, you could get burned by this fire. This might hurt.* She shut out the voice of reason in her head. Her flesh craved instant gratification. Throwing all caution to the wind, she silenced the warning voice in her head.

Stuck in the throes of passion, she couldn't bear the thought of losing that brief moment of pleasure. Even if she got only 30 minutes of Beba's smiling at her, kissing and caressing her. She ran her fingers through his hair as he planted feathery kisses on her breasts and her navel. His wet tongue circled round her navel and an alarm went off in her head. *When and how had he get to my navel?* Her ankle-length Vlisco dress was pushed up around her stomach.

Breathlessly, she muttered, "This isn't going to happen."

Tears spilled from her eyes and trickled down her cheeks. Beba raised his head and looked at her.

"You're beautiful," he said, kissing every inch of her face, tasting the saltiness on her cheeks.

Love is pain. What if I wake up regretting this?

Cupping his flushed face in her hand, she pushed him away.

"Let's not make the goodbyes more difficult than necessary," she said.

He sighed, hugging her close. His warm breath raised up every strand of hair at the nape of her neck.

"I don't want to say goodbye," he whispered. "But I don't want to make any promises."

She pulled herself out of his grip and looked at him. Did that mean she had to be strong? She willed herself to try, to try to protect herself. Hadn't her mantra always been: 'It's every woman's duty to protect herself?'

"I know," she said. She rose, straightened her gown and opened the door. Common sense told her it was time to let the bird fly away. If this bird came back, then she would know it was meant to be. Yet, inside she was hurting.

Beba stepped out of the door. He couldn't take his eyes off her.

"I don't want us to part on a sour note. Let's ... we need to ..."

Beba ran his fingers through his hair. That single act made her heart race faster. Why hasn't she foreseen, in the beginning, that he could make her shiver for no reason at all? Why had she ignored the premonition that Beba was capable – in a single wave of his hand – of turning her to mush?

Looking at him, she sensed that he too was in a dilemma. She felt that, when he made this arrangement, he wanted only to find his mother. Not love. And there she was fighting back tears, trying to be strong.

In one swift movement, she pulled off the engagement ring, and thrust it into his palm.

"Here," she said.

"What? No, no. It's ..."

"It's over, isn't it?"

"Keep it. It's a gift. Please don't do this." He cupped her hands in his and gently slid the ring back on her finger.

"I'll do an electronic transfer tomorrow," he said.

"No need. The arrangement didn't eat into my work time," she replied, wondering if she had to slap some sense into his head to make him see that it wasn't his money she cared about.

"An agreement is an agreement. I said I'd pay for the time you worked."

She shut the door. From the window, she saw him standing there with his raised hand, preparing to knock. When his hand fell to his side, she knew he had changed his mind.

Thirteen

"Kambi The Love Goddess signing out. Stay tuned for the news at nine from Love 100.5 FM. Let's meet here same time tomorrow evening. Goodnight."

Kambi removed her headphones and took a deep breath. Through the studio window, she could see DJ Upbeat getting ready to play a song during the break before the news.

The disc jockey looked at her and saw her thumbs up, cheering him on. He smiled and nodded. Pushing her chair back, she rose. She tucked her blue file in her bag and sighed. Her head ached.

Chaka Khan's *Ain't Nobody* sounded in the studio. She smiled. The song was her personal favourite. Now, hearing Chaka Khan's voice wailing those words transported her back to the moments she had spent with Beba.

After having spent most of her time since parting from him revising the poems, she was able to control the urge to see him, to kiss him. Almost fifty poems penned down and memories of him remained fresh in her mind.

She was free, but not as happy as she'd expected. Tima was out there in the book publishing world, trying to negotiate a deal with a publisher. Kambi didn't know what to expect from the unpredictable publishing business. There were no guarantees. It didn't matter that her agent had gushed over the poems, especially the haiku verses. She could only hope for the best. Completing the manuscript made her feel wonderful.

Could I have done it without him? Perhaps. Beba had made the trip much more exciting for her. But with the end of the romance came a dull ache in her heart. Her legs weakened when she remembered him. Sometimes, she grew angry with herself and even angry at Beba, for putting her through such emotional turmoil and then walking away afterwards.

Strolling beside the line of cars stuck in a traffic jam, she thought back to her first kiss with Beba.

Where is he now? What is he doing? Does he think of me as much as I think of him?

She tried to shake thoughts of him from her mind. It was eight days since they'd said their goodbyes. Why hadn't the heartache faded?

Two blocks from the glass-walled, two-storey radio house, she dialled his number again. It was unreachable. Hissing, she frowned. She had kept both her holiday and regular phone lines active, but Beba hadn't phoned.

In the beginning, she had expected that it would be easy to forget his smile, his piercing eyes, and his voice. And he had called shortly after she had left the resort, but Kambi neither answered nor returned his calls. She had hoped that snubbing him would hasten the process of forgetting him. But it hadn't worked out that way.

Tossing her smartphone into her big handbag, she

crossed the road and walked towards BountyBites.

Kaycee had invited Kambi to meet her there to celebrate God-knows-what. Kaycee was like that, always looking for a reason to celebrate.

People trooped in and out of BountyBites clutching plastic bags, talking and chatting. Kambi walked in and climbed up the stairs. Kaycee had been specific in her description – upstairs, by the window.

"Kambi, over here!" a familiar voice called. Kambi saw the waving hand before she saw Diana shining with an inexplicable happiness. What had changed her so much, Kambi wondered. Sitting next to Diana was Kaycee, who was looking over her shoulder and winking at Kambi.

"Diana, how are the twins?" Kambi asked.

Diana nodded. "They're fine. They're with their father now."

"I've been meaning to come to your place but work pressure ..." Kambi said, as she hugged her sister. Turning to Kaycee, she said, "Fashionista, what are you doing in PH?" Slowly, she removed her handbag and tossed it under the table.

Diana began apologising for the long silence, but she paused when Kaycee started saying, "Business and boyfriend."

Diana raised her eyebrows questioningly. And Kaycee rephrased her response.

"Did I say boyfriend? Forgive me." Kaycee placed her left hand on the table and wriggled her ring finger.

"Pararapaparaaaa!" she shrieked.

Kambi blocked her ears. From the corner of her eyes, she could see that many people were staring at them.

Oh, let them look. Why can't they mind their food? The least she could do was jig-dance with her friend. So she pushed back her chair, oohing and aahing as she rose.

"Tonye the architect finally put a ring on it. After five years of off-and-on loving," Kambi said, as she twirled around. Her heart felt lighter now there was good news to take her mind off Beba and the pending book contract.

"Tonye weds Kaycee. It's about time you two stepped up your game," Diana added, sipping her Fanta. Divorced 30-year-old that she was, she had a keen interest in blossoming love relationships. "Speaking of engagements ... Kambi, why aren't you wearing your ring?" Diana said.

Kambi frowned and shook her head. "It's not. It wasn't..."

"I heard you met a miracle worker. You went up that mountain single and in two weeks you were engaged," Diana said. She folded her arms across her chest as she stared coolly at her younger sister. Kambi sensed Diana's displeasure at her strange secretiveness, and shrugged.

"You seem to have heard more than you ought to know. I am not in the mood to make a case for myself," Kambi said, smiling.

She missed confiding in her sister, but how was she supposed to explain that the engagement was all stage-managed? It wouldn't make any sense to them. She suspected that Diana wouldn't believe her, especially if she told them that she had sold the engagement ring and used the money towards schools fee for a charity she supported.

"It's been a while, Kambi. I'm sorry, but I've been very busy these past few weeks. Work and life and ..." Diana paused, and looked at both of them. Kambi suspected that she'd just managed to stop herself from giving too much information. Why was her sister smiling shyly? What was she hiding? Why were her eyes bright and hopeful? Diana's eyes had been tired and sunken back when she was going through her divorce. Had she started seeing someone, Kambi wondered.

Trying to divert everyone's attention, Kambi said, "You didn't miss me."

"Little sis, I did. Really. It's complicated."

"Uncomplicate it then," Kaycee chipped in. Having grown up as an only child, she'd always been envious of Kambi and Diana's relationship.

"Neither of you will understand. Kambi, what did you bring back from the mountain?" Diana asked, grinning from ear to ear. Her dimples sank deeper into her cheeks. Her dark brown skin gleamed like a polished ebony sculpture.

"Print wax materials," Kambi replied.

"I hope you bought some for Mum. She's been looking forward to seeing you. I told her about your new guy. She seemed excited. But she's worried. Why are you shutting her out?" Diana asked. She touched Kambi's shaky hand.

"Kambi, are you still upset with your mother?" Kaycee asked.

Kambi shook her head. *Don't they understand? Anger didn't drive me away from family. It was shame.*

"I was angry, but not so much. I was even more ashamed. I felt like a failure," Kambi replied. Her voice was low. Distancing herself from family hadn't been easy at all. She missed them but she wanted to prove that she could be successful at something, if not relationships and marriage. The publishing deal, she had hoped, would give her the confidence she sought. But now she wasn't so sure.

Diana leaned closer to the table and asked, "What do you have to be ashamed of? You did your best to make the relationship work, didn't you?" Kambi nodded. "Why are you being hard on yourself? Things go wrong. There's nothing to be ashamed of. I'm 30 and divorced. Should I spend the rest of my life hugging high voltage transformers?"

Kaycee touched Kambi's shoulder. "Please, go and visit your mother," she said. "Diana will accompany you. Life is short."

Look at the lengths Beba had to go to in order to find his mother ... You have but one life to live and so does your mother.

Diana shrugged.

"Now that we're done with the intervention, let's get back to the Obudu gist," Kaycee said, grinning from ear to ear. "Kambi, what happened between you and the fine guy? I told you to hold on to that good man; they're hard to come by."

Diana thrust her fist in the air, "Yes! I am a witness."

Kambi looked at both of them and said, "Agreement happened." She clicked her tongue and added, "Forget it." Her head dropped.

"Anyway, Tonye and I already fixed the date. Next month. I don't know why Tonye's in a hurry," Kaycee prattled. "Kambi, I want you to be my maid of honour."

Kambi's jaw dropped. Why me? she almost yelled, but she didn't want to be a wet blanket. So she focused on the positive side of things. She had enjoyed being Diana's maid of honour. She'd got so caught up in the excitement of the wedding that she'd almost felt like the bride. Nowadays, she was nervous of nuptials; they reminded her of the experience of her botched wedding and of Diana's failed marriage.

What if something went wrong? I don't want to jinx Kaycee's big day.

Kambi imagined another upside to being maid of honour. She could help plan her friend's wedding and even read a poem during the toast.

And it will take my mind off this whole book deal business and Beba.

"Of course, I'll be your maid of honour," Kambi said, smiling.

"As if you had a choice," Kaycee joked. Her bangles jangled. Her weave bounced as she shook her head. Kambi stared as Kaycee rubbed her palms and continued talking about her plans.

Her phone announced the arrival of a text message. Kambi looked at the phone. Her heart skipped two beats. The text message was from her agent. It read:

I HAVE NEWS FOR YOU. MEET ME AT MY OFFICE AT 12 NOON, MONDAY.

Fourteen

Kambi ran down the dark and unfamiliar street. She had never seen the old brick houses that stood on either side. A dog barked in the distance and stopped. They were still running after her; she'd seen half a dozen of them wearing masks and black capes. Her fists clenched as she raced down the block.

The ground became colder as she ran. She could feel the chills creeping up her spine. Further down, the rest of the road was paved with hard, glistening ice. She slowed down, panting.

Suddenly, a large hand pulled her into a well-lit alleyway. She squealed and whipped out her pocketknife.

"Don't do it!" It was a man's voice, a familiar voice. A closer look at his face revealed his identity – Beba. He smiled at her and said, "Let's get out of here."

Kambi woke up, sweating. It had been a dream. What a dream! Lately, her mind had been playing games. She sat up in bed and tried to clear her head. Only one day to go and she would meet her agent to hear the news. She hoped it'd be good news, but she didn't want to worry about it.

The ticking clock drew her eyes to the wall: 5.30am. Diana had convinced her that she should visit their parents' home later that day. It was an intervention to get Kambi to reconcile with their mother. Kambi knew, but didn't try to fight it.

Anger was eating at her heart and soul: a clear sign that it was time to make peace with her mother.

Her parents used to be a source of comfort and refuge, but things had changed since the events of the failed wedding.

*****

She drove through the tree-lined streets of GRA Phase 1, looking out for the repainted orange gate that marked her parents' house. It used to be a black one with the number 30 glazed over it, but Diana had told her that her parents had decided to change the colour of the gate. Some of the neighbours had changed the colours of theirs too.

Kambi sang along to the song on the sound system. Her mind was plagued with thoughts of the brief romance she'd shared with Beba and the book deal.

She found the orange gate with the bougainvillea hedge and hooted. The security man opened the gate and she realised how much she had missed the company of family.

Pulling up in the driveway, she crooned along to Fergie's *Big Girls Don't Cry*. The coda of the song brought tears to her eyes. The song had soothed her soul, but not as much as she had expected. Her heart still craved the man who was at the other end of the continent, searching for his mother. And here she was, in front of her own mother's house, wondering what to say to her after ten months of estrangement.

Kambi remembered how she had considered herself as one who had been raised by a single mother even though her father had never left them. And how different things had been lately. For the past few months, she had grown closer to her father.

Her father was a highlife musician, and she saw him as something of a rolling stone. Her earliest memories had involved her father coming and going so often that she imagined he was a concerned uncle whom her mother had been fond of, an uncle who enjoyed teaching her to play the saxophone. Things had changed after her 13th birthday. Her father, too old to keep up with the frequent travelling, returned home to play his music locally and that was when she and her sister had started to build a relationship with him.

Her father greeted her at the door with a hug. Diana yelled from somewhere in the kitchen. The house smelled of boiling meat and chopped onions and green vegetables. Kambi joined her in the kitchen and asked about their mother. "She is stuck in traffic, but she'll be home soon," Diana said. She placed a pot of waterleaves on the fire.

Diana's twin sons ran into the kitchen, holding tin drums and screaming, "Auntie Ambi, Auntie Ambi!"

Kambi hugged them. The tips of their fez caps pressed against Kambi's legs. She lifted them one after the other and said, "You're both so big now. What has Mummy been feeding you?"

"Daddy bought us chocolates," Ayobami said.

"And ice cream!" Ayodeji added. They both giggled and ran off to play.

Kambi laughed and turned to Diana. "You're doing a good job with them. I see Femi has been spoiling them."

Diana sighed. "Kambi, I have been wanting to tell you something."

"I'm all ears," Kambi replied. She'd had to bite her lips to keep from exclaiming, "I knew there was something."

"Kambi, don't judge me, but I am falling in love again."

"That's not entirely a bad thing," Kambi replied.

"It's my ex. I'm seeing my ex-husband," she said.

"Who? Femi? Beyond spending time with the boys?" Kambi asked. She cocked her head to the left and asked, "Is that why you've been excited lately?"

Diana nodded, and frowned.

"How long has this been going on?" Kambi looked into Diana's shining face and saw that she was definitely happier than she'd been in a long time. When was the last time she'd ever seen her so radiant?

Kambi poured some palm oil into the pot of boiling waterleaves as Diana's reply hit her: "Six months. Eight months. Dunno. It's crazy. Divorced four years and we're sneaking around. We can't even remember what we were fighting about."

Kambi was thinking about their break-up. They'd handled it maturely, had said they were parting due to 'irreconcilable conflicts'. Diana had thrown herself into her bank work, and Femi spent days and nights at his hospital. They were both cut up about it, but neither had resorted to fighting over the kids or mudslinging or backbiting. Kambi had expected them to fight dirty, but they didn't. Femi was reasonable and gentle with Diana, even when she was touchy.

"I don't know, Diana. Are you sure you shouldn't give it time before announcing it?"

Diana cleared her throat. "Perhaps," she said, "but he says he wants us to formalise our union again, you know. Kambi, I think he's changed."

"People don't change," their father's hoarse voice cut in. His speaking voice was quite different from the velvety baritone with which he sang his highlife music. He stood behind them and continued: "What if he's the same man you've always known him to be? Would you still love him or want to stay married to him? Femi's just a bit more mature."

Kambi and Diana exchanged glances: a silent agreement that their father had some shocking – yet interesting – things to say. Diana exhaled. Kambi turned to sprinkle some onions, crayfish and seasoning into the soup.

The twins showed up with their tin drums, old beverage cans recovered from the kitchen bin.

"The Grand ol' Duke of York!" Ayodeji sang, adeptly wielding his drumsticks.

"He had 10,000 men!" Ayobami beamed, chanting as

he watched his brother. He drummed a tin-tyn-tin-tyn with him.

Momentarily waving their sticks they chanted: "And when they were up, they were up; and when they were down, they were down ..."

Though their drumming was quite noisy, Kambi giggled at their ingenuity.

"How many times have I warned you not to play in the kitchen?" their mother said. "I'll report you to Grandma."

"No. I'm sorry, Mummy," Ayobami cried.

But Ayodeji said, "You can tell her if you like. She's not back yet!"

"Don't speak to your mother like that!" their grandfather said, shooing them away with his hands.

Ayodeji frowned. His eyes welled up with tears. The twins both shuffled out of the kitchen.

***

Thirty minutes later, Kambi sighed and looked at her watch.

Her father rubbed her shoulder and said, "I just got off the phone with your mother, she'll soon be home. She is so excited."

Kambi paused, and remembered the gentle way he had said, "You were lucky to get away, Kambi. That Victor had no love in his heart for you." She'd been surprised to hear those words from him only two days after the aborted wedding.

Now, Kambi watched as his tall figure leaned into the sink. Sunlight streamed into the kitchen, throwing patterns across his back.

"I look forward to seeing her too," Kambi started to say. The kettle of water began whistling on the gas cooker. "But let's talk about Diana's confusion. And love. What if Femi genuinely loves her?"

Diana lifted the kettle and poured the water into a bowl of garri.

"Look, I'm in no position to lecture you about love. Because hey, I was hardly here for your mother, and four of your siblings died, but I chose to be out there on the road. It's possible that Femi loves her. Remember the famous quote 'love is what two people have been through?'" He paused and took a deep breath. Kambi sighed and so did Diana. His eyes shone with guilt and shame even though he was too proud to apologise.

"Papa, why does something as beautiful as love have to be complicated?" Diana asked.

Their father nodded his head as though in a moment of introspection. He moved to the fridge, walking across the dappled patches of sunlight on the tiled floor. Kambi poured the ground afang leaves into the pot and stirred. Diana carried a bowl of garri into the dining room. Kambi began to add the boiled meat into the soup.

"I don't have all the answers." He stood at the entrance of the dining room. "I feel guilty that you've had bad relationships because I didn't provide an example of how a good man should treat a woman he loves," he said.

Kambi's hand froze. She looked at Diana, whose mouth was hanging open.

"I hope it's not too late. I mean, much damage has been done. And you're both women. Kambi, 24, almost 25, and Diana, 30. God, time flies."

They heard their mother's Peugeot 405 pull into the driveway. Kambi frowned.

"That's Mrs Emem Obi driving in. Kambi, remember she loves you. She regrets trying to arrange that marriage with Victor," her father said. His tone was hushed. He walked over to unlock the door. His movements were measured, yet agile. At 65, he had the energy of a twenty-something-year-old.

Mrs Emem Obi was the name their father jocularly called his wife. Kambi looked at him, the rolling stone whose rugged face became more handsome as age touched it. She went into the kitchen and turned off the cooker. She ladled the soup into a ceramic serving dish. Diana came over and hugged her. "Our mother means well, has always meant well. Don't you know?" Diana whispered.

"I know," Kambi said. She placed the bowl of soup on the dining table and looked up. Her mother was standing at the doorway, tears streaming down her cheeks. She was mouthing Kambi's name with quivering lips.

"Momma," Kambi said as she walked towards her mother.

The older woman was so slender, so fragile-looking that Kambi was careful to hug her gently.

"I'm sorry," Kambi cried as she patted her mother's hair. "I didn't mean to shut you out. I was angry and ashamed."

"Why? Why, you had nothing to be ashamed of. I'm sorry too. I haven't been able to forgive myself for agreeing to introduce you to Victor," their mother said.

Kambi breathed deeply. Nothing mattered now. She felt a weight lifting off her chest.

***

The twins were dozing off on their grandparents' bed when lunch was served.

Once the adults had settled down to lunch, Kambi looked across the table and smiled. Her mother was biting off a piece of fish and chewing with relish.

"So how was your trip to Obudu?" her mother asked, as she moulded another ball of garri.

"Fine. I rested and completed a project I've been working on."

"How's your poetry going?"

Kambi nodded. "So-so," she said.

"And the man you met? Diana said some interesting things about him," her mother said. She was smiling her wide smile, showing the gap teeth Kambi had always admired.

"The man is an old friend. We're just friends. But since

Diana has more interesting—"

Diana nudged Kambi with her elbow to hush her. Their mother watched them both and shook her head. Their father hummed as he ate; he was lost in a world of his own. The rest of the family was used to it. Her mother waited until she'd emptied her plate of garri and soup before she said, "So what does this friend do for a living?"

"He owns a mining company and a winery."

"Sounds like an ambitious man. I hope he's much older?"

Kambi frowned and nodded. "But age is just a number, Ma."

"I've always believed the older the better." Her mother washed her hands.

Their father cleared his throat. "Your mother has funny ideas about what guarantees a successful relationship." There was a tone of finality to his voice.

Diana banged on the table and paused as though she regretted the banging. "Stop talking as though our mother knows nothing about love," she fumed.

"Good God," Kambi muttered. Very typical of Diana, she thought. Diana was the outrageous one, the party-rocker, with the razor-sharp mouth. Their mother used to say that Diana had inherited the razor-mouth from her Ibibio mother. Kambi was the reader, the poet, the soft-spoken, tender daughter. She sipped from her glass of water and swallowed hard. Everyone hoped the boys wouldn't awake from their sleep.

"She waited for you, worked hard raising your kids while you were out sowing your wild oats!" Diana yelled.

"Young lady! Do not speak to me in that manner," their father said, his fist punching the air; his voice wavered somewhere between high and low. It was high enough to shock Diana, to shut her up, and low enough to make Kambi's "Here we go again" audible.

They stared at him in silence for a while. Then the girls turned to their mother. They were expecting her to smash a glass on the wall, as she would have done when they were much younger. Now, she just stared at her husband, frowning.

"Forgive me," he said. "Your mother is a strong woman but she has bad taste in men."

Kambi stabbed a piece of meat with her toothpick. Their mother was obviously not in the mood for a fight.

Their mother lifted her hand and said, "Enough! Diana, don't talk to your father like that. And Kambi, let's talk in the garden."

***

Oyster and periwinkle shells crunched under their feet as they made their way to the swinging chair. They sat down and listened to birdsong from the fruit trees. The mild afternoon sun danced on the leaves of the trees and threw patterns on the chair, the grass and the ixora and hibiscus flowers.

"You like the Obudu man a lot, don't you?" her mother asked.

"Well, yes. I do."

"You have to be careful this time around. I don't want you to get hurt," Her mother said.

"Now, you're sounding like our father."

"There's some truth in what your father said. You should listen to your heart, but think with your head. Not the other way around. There's no mathematics or science about matters of the heart."

"Hmm. 'The heart has reasons that reason cannot know' – Blaise Pascal. Now, I'm thinking it explains why you stayed with our father."

"I don't try to rationalise these things," her mother said. "It's like trying to explain Diana's sneaking around with Femi."

"You've known all along?" Kambi asked.

"Of course, I knew from day one. She's my daughter, isn't she? I know when she's down and when she's happy. I know when she's falling in love and when she's falling out of love."

"But how did you know it was him?"

"I didn't go prying. I just stumbled upon some evidence." Her mother picked up a flower stalk. "Besides, he's probably the only one who can understand and put up with her."

Kambi sighed. "Let's hope it works out for the good."

"That's the thing with love. You can only hope. But you can't keep running from it. You have to give it a shot."

Kambi remembered Beba and how she'd resisted him.

Had she driven him away? The possibility scared her. Yet, she was angry with herself for needing another person so much. Could she call it love, she wondered.

"But love hurts," she said, squeezing her mother's hand. "The uncertainty can be numbing. You know ... not knowing how it'll work out. It makes me wonder, what's the point of it all?"

"Kambi, fear is a near-useless emotion. Don't let it rob you of your chance to live." Her mother pulled her closer. Kambi leaned on her shoulder and sighed.

Diana's voice reverberated through the house as she shouted: "Don't play with your food!"

Kambi and her mother looked at each other and knew that the twins were awake.

Fifteen

The search for his mother hadn't been as easy as he had expected. The South African media had taken up his cause and announced that a love child – a coloured man – had arrived at the O.R. Tambo International Airport from Nigeria, in search of his mother – Marie, as the retired general called her.

Aged men and women, white and black alike, approached him with claims of having sent their children to faraway lands in order to escape the wrath of the apartheid government. Beba listened and marvelled at how special their experiences were.

Though he drew strength from their stories, he worried that none of them was Marie. Each night, he retired to his suite at the Premier Hotel feeling tired, and wondering whether he'd ever find his mother.

The trips to the address his father had given him hadn't yielded the results he'd hoped for.

Beba learned that Marie's family had long moved out of their flat; and that she had married and divorced, and remarried. Beba took long taxi drives through the large city while the taxi driver regaled him with tales about 'Johustleburg'. One day, he went to the University of the Witwatersrand, where his father had been studying when he'd met Marie.

From time to time, he distracted himself with Kambi's

blog, *Diary of a Jilted Bride*. Beba read each poem, digested each line of poetry, searching for solace, for clues.

Occasionally, he extended his search to Facebook and Twitter to see if Kambi had reactivated her Facebook account, but to no avail. Visiting her blog every half-hour, he learned of Kambi's anxiety. Would her agent like her poetry collections or not? He often left anonymous comments, encouraging her to be strong, promising never to reject her. Later, it dawned on him that she was more afraid of a rejection from a publisher. He became more aware of her changing emotions – her doubts and fears. He wished he could stretch out his arms to comfort her, but they were were half a continent apart. And he was busy coming to terms with the circumstances surrounding his birth.

On the third day of Beba's visit, a round-faced porter knocked at his hotel door and gave him a brown envelope. He gave him a tip and thanked him. Then, he shut the door and tore open the envelope. His hand shook as he pulled out a hand-written letter and a picture – it was a copy of the same picture he had. Beba studied the spidery squiggle as he read, "If you have a copy of this picture and more proof, come to the address on the envelope, tomorrow."

The next day, he booked a flight from Johannesburg to Cape Town.

He spent his entire time at the hotel replying to e-mails,

giving orders and analysing reports from his offices. But his time on the plane was spent dreaming. His mind often drifted to Kambi. Beba exhaled heavily and closed his laptop. *I can't do any work. All I think about is her.* He glanced at his watch and shut his eyes. *She's just finished her programme and she's giving a thumbs up to the next host. She'll either go to her sister's or call her agent. By now, she has news from the publisher.* Beba rubbed his temples. *Why do I always do that? What does that make me? Lovestruck?* He tried to look out of the window, but all he saw was her reflection, stealing the glass where his should be.

Beba got off the flight and hailed a taxi. A cool breeze blew in his face as the taxi sped off to the address he'd handed to the driver. As the taxi screeched to a halt, Beba alighted and handed the driver a wad of notes.

After briefly surveying the upscale neighbourhood, he knocked. He waited before he knocked again and again, until the solid door of the large old house nearly cracked his fingers. No-one answered the door. He stepped back and looked up. An old man was watching him through one of the windows.

"Who are you looking for?" he barked, scratching his balding head.

Too tired to shout his intentions, Beba took in his light-skinned face. The old man wore a white, crisp shirt, black trousers and braces. His clean-shaven face gleamed in the mid-afternoon sun. He didn't want to attract any more attention to himself. Fishing the photograph from his diary, he held it up for the curious man to see. "Marie," Beba mouthed.

"It's you," said the man. He was grinning toothlessly. "Good, you came early. She's at Arcadia. It's an old people's home, right next to Groote Schuur Hospital. On the slopes of Devil's Peak." The man waved and disappeared behind the curtains.

Beba wrote down the address and got in another taxi.

***

Beba found his mother stretched on a bed. She was fast asleep.

Marie looked handsome and peaceful, even though time and age had etched lines of sorrow on her face. Beba introduced himself to Judy, Marie's only daughter. He showed them pictures and letters that had been exchanged between his father and their mother.

"How sad that you should come now," said Judy. "She has Alzheimer's disease. She can't even remember her own children."

Beba stared at Judy. She looked just like the lady in the picture he'd been carrying about.

"I am glad to have found her alive," Beba said, sighing. He touched the woman's long veined arms and brushed strands of hair off her face.

Marie opened her eyes and sat up.

"Mom," Judy called, hesitantly. She propped a pillow against the wall and helped Marie lean on it. But Marie stood and wobbled towards her rocking chair. Beba stepped around the bed and helped her sit.

"Thank you," she said, staring hard at him. Pointing at him, she said, "I know you. You're the Nigerian undergraduate at Wits." Marie grinned, propping up her chin with her palms.

Beba smiled. "That was my father," he said. Did she have any memories of his birth?

The woman stared at him, brows creased. Judy turned to Beba, then to Marie.

Outside, people walked about, pushing wheelchairs; others carried trays of drugs. The place had an antiseptic smell.

"Mom, you need to rest," Judy said to Marie, while keeping an eye on Beba. "You need to eat and take your medicine."

"I know. I know. I'll rest." Marie leaned back in her rocking chair and sniffed. Did she remember anything? Beba shrugged.

"Could you please leave for a while?" Judy asked. "Come back later. She wouldn't like to eat with strangers around." Beba tensed at the sound of her low, pleading voice.

"No. No. Let him stay," the woman said. Her feeble hand waved him on. Beba sat and watched her eat oatmeal. She chewed and swallowed without a fuss. Occasionally, her blue eyes darted and stared at Beba. But she didn't say anything. She frowned and groaned as Judy handed her the medicine.

"Drink, Mom," she said. Marie swallowed some pills and threw the others on the floor. Judy sighed. "What was that for?" she said.

Beba sat there watching the women until Marie drifted into another peaceful sleep. He left the home, having learned of two half-brothers who would visit later.

Back at his hotel room, he thought of his newly found family. Marie probably couldn't remember that she'd had him. What was the point in staying on? His heart was heavy with grief and longing.

He thought of Kambi. Memories of her laughter and kiss plagued his mind like a persistent ghost. Why couldn't he shake her off? Everything flummoxed him – the strange feeling of incompleteness he felt, even as he had stood in front of the recently discovered Marie, holding her thin hand. He couldn't ignore the stirring in his heart – the realisation that, if Kambi had not come into the picture, his mother might have died before he met her.

A day after visiting Marie, he woke up to the jarring ring of his mobile phone. Mina was crying at the other end of the line, explaining that his vineyard had caught fire. Beba listened carefully. He could hear the administrator and the farmers screaming as they poured buckets of water over the vines. He hung up and dialled the local fire service. They complained that the roads were bad. They probably wouldn't get there until afternoon.

He dressed, packed his bags and left the room. Twice in the taxi, he dialled Kambi's number, but then hung up.

There was so much going on in his life, he wanted to get some comfort from her voice. But he didn't want to bother her. Since he arrived in South Africa, he had called her several times but he would hang up after she had said a good number of hellos. Once, she had yelled 'sicko' down the phone.

Yes, he was lovesick.

The taxi dropped him off at the hospital. He wrestled his luggage up to his mother's room. A young man sat next to her bed patting Marie's hand, cajoling her to take her medicine. Marie swung her head from side to side chanting, "No, no, no ..."

Beba smiled. "Good morning. My name is Beba. I'm visiting from Nigeria." He held out his hand. Holding the pills in a saucer, the young man shook his hand.

"Michael," he replied. "Judy told me about your visit yesterday."

Beba nodded. They talked about Marie's failing health, about their jobs and ambitions. Beba explained that his vineyard had caught fire, and he was afraid that his winery would suffer. Michael was sympathetic.

Marie woke up intermittently, called Beba's name and drifted off into a new round of sleep. At one point, Michael said, "You think she knows who you are?"

"Er, I'm not sure. I think it's my father she remembers. My father and I bear the same names though. I have junior after mine."

They were quiet for a while. Then Michael said, "She doesn't remember any of us. It's sad, I don't feel I got to know her enough before the Alzheimer's struck. I felt even guiltier when our father passed on. We never got along."

"I understand, man," Beba said, clutching Michael's shoulder. "You need to forgive yourself."

When Michael tried to feed her, Marie fought him, her lips pressed tight together. She brushed off his hands, almost knocking the glass of water out of his hand. Michael pleaded with her. She groaned. Beba recorded everything with a video camera. He would probably show his father when he got home. But the old man still had Eunice.

"I must leave now," Beba said.

Michael handed him his business card and said, "Keep in touch. We should hang out soon." Beba nodded, left the hospital and headed straight for the airport.

***

Beba flew back to Johannesburg. He bowed his head in disappointment when he learned that his flight leaving for Nigeria the next morning had been delayed.

This time, he checked into a room in D'Oreale Grande Hotel. It was close to the airport, and he'd recently read good reviews about it.

Surprised to find that he wasn't feeling as exhausted as he'd expected, he began to attend to business. He was glad that the fire trucks had arrived quickly. A small part of the vineyard had been damaged but the winery could still produce as much quality wine as before.

But there was still the question of Kambi. Did she get the book deal? Who was she celebrating her success with? He read all the new poems on her blog. Initially, he was relieved to find that the tone was light-hearted and warm, as though she was in love. Who were the love poems about? He became agitated. What if she'd found someone? His heart skipped a beat. He was concerned that she hadn't mentioned the book deal. Had it worked out well?

There was no way to tell. She had only announced that she would be giving a private poetry performance at her friend's wedding at Cyprian's Church, where she was to be maid of honour.

He looked in the mirror and winked: Beba, the internet stalker! He spread his arms and fell backwards into his bed. He soon fell asleep.

On the plane back to Nigeria, Beba decided that he needed to know her position. Did she believe they could start a real relationship? From her blog posts, he could tell that she had enjoyed her time at the Obudu Mountain Resort. But there was no way to know what she wanted. Was she commitment-phobic? Would she give him another chance to prove that he wanted to wake up every morning to see her dishevelled braids? Much as he suspected that she would feel embarrassed, he enjoyed ruffling her hair anyway. But he had to ask her, to convince her. She had resisted him so many times, but he wouldn't give up.

Then he thought about his mother, slipping into death's arms. Hadn't he learned about the ephemerality of life?

I am rich, but my millions can't buy time. Making the most of every moment is a virtue. First, I must bare my heart to Kambi. I don't want to have the kind of regrets Michael has.

Beba's breath quickened as he imagined crashing the wedding at St Cyprian's Church ...

No, it wouldn't come to that. I can cheer her on: she will make a very attractive maid of honour.

Now he pictured himself in the crowd, clapping and shouting her name. In his imagination, he followed her everywhere. At some point, she threatened to spray him away with a canister of pesticide. He jerked out of his reverie, flushing with embarrassment. He wanted her, desperately, and he had to let her know. How would he know what his chances were, if he didn't try?

"We shall be landing at the Murtala Muhammed Airport in ten minutes ..." a mechanical voice cackled. Beba sighed in relief. He was tired, yet he tried to stay hopeful. "Everything will be fine," he muttered as he looked out of the window at the stretch of rusting aluminium roofs amidst greenery and water.

Sixteen

As at most memorable weddings, the choristers' voices rose in beautiful cadences, the priest bellowed his sermon, and everyone else – bride, groom, bridal party and guests – sat quietly in the pews.

Kambi couldn't trust herself to behave until the time for the exchanging of the vows. But she managed to stay calm and collected throughout.

Bouquet and veil in hands, she watched Kaycee and her groom make those everlasting promises of love to each other. And she realised that such a promise as this to Victor would have been lies in the long run. *Good thing he didn't show up*. The marriage would certainly have been a very lonely one. She imagined herself, living in his big house, constantly filled with a sense of dread.

Miles away from here, Kambi had experienced true joy and love with the most unlikely person. She stood at the altar watching the couple exchange rings. *I had the time of my life at Obudu*. Smiles played across her lips as memories of Beba's kiss came flooding into her mind. *It was magical*. But why did she let pride stop her from expressing her emotions? *How long will you deprive yourself of joy?*

"You may now kiss the bride," the priest said gently.

The groom bent his knee, pulled his bride closer and kissed her. A round of applause erupted from the congregation. Catcalls filled the air. The wedding march emanated from the organ. And Kambi thought of Beba's guitar strings. His soulful melodies. She looked back, into the crowd. Her eyes caught a man with a mop of dark curly hair, neatly parted at the side. *Am I imagining things?* She had seen his blue eyes, unmistakably Beba's lovely blue eyes. Likely his mother's eyes – given that Kambi had seen his father's bold black eyes. Kambi looked back again. Just to be sure.

Sure enough, it was him. He winked at her and laughed. Mouth agape, she watched him run his finger through his hair, and she had to look away to keep from running into his arms.

Everything has gone well, so far. Kambi, if you create a scene and steal the bride's thunder, she will never forgive you.

But why did her heart pound with anticipation? Only Beba had that power over her. Her anger seemed to have eluded her.

Oh, I mustn't be distracted from the task at hand, I have travelled all the way to Calabar for one thing – to be maid of honour; and I have to do my best not to dishonour the bride.

"Go in peace ..." the priest began to say. Kambi tuned him out and began to gather the frills of the bride's gown. The newly wedded couple held hands and danced down the aisle behind the procession of priests.

Kambi peeked at Beba from the corner of her eye. His cream-coloured suit made him stand out. She felt strange stirrings ... it was everything: his smile, his composure, the glint in his eyes.

Kambi chided herself. Just as she took the next step, she lost her balance and stumbled. But she was quick to smile and strut forward to recover her posture; she hoped no-one had noticed.

Kaycee turned, flashing a wide smile. "Oh my God, there are so many people here," she said, holding Kambi's hand.

They were standing in front of the certificates. Tonye was appending his signature to the documents.

"Yes, and they're as excited as you are," Kambi replied, giving her hand a reassuring squeeze.

Kaycee smiled.

"I saw one oyinbo guy who resembles your Obudu boyfriend. The mixed-race guy – what's his name again? – who took us to Tinapa?"

Kambi blinked at her and smiled, "Sign your documents jor. Join the procession; dance with your new husband. It's your day," she said.

Kaycee grinned and wagged her finger as though she suspected Kambi of something. The crowd cheered as she signed the documents. Kambi leaned over, spreading the veil over Kaycee's shoulder.

Kambi heaved a sigh of relief as soon as the bride stood, slung her arm through the groom's and danced out of the church.

***

Beba Sambe felt it again: the uncontrollable urge to hold Kambi, to kiss her. Desperately, passionately – to swoop her off to the back seat of his car for five minutes, at least.

She had bowled him over. From the moment he saw her behind the bride, his heart did an uncontrollable triple somersault. He had to admit it: she looked drop-dead gorgeous in her pink, fitted, ankle-length gown. And her hair had been pulled in an onion-like bun to one side of her head. Her face was radiant, dark and beautiful; her glistening light pink lips made him shiver. Little wonder, he had to clamp down the urge to kiss her.

Elbowing his way through the throng of guests, he apologised when he stepped on the foot of an irate guest. He decided that he had to get to her, whatever it took. It hurt to watch her helping the bride into the car.

Beba prayed, even though he hadn't prayed in a long time. *Dear Lord, let Kambi love me in return.*

He walked, waving his hands in the air. Kambi was climbing into the decorated Jeep, alongside the bride and the little girl in white. Beba's heart sank with grief. So much hopelessness rose within him that he screamed her name, as a drowning man would cry for help.

"Kambi! Please wait!"

He hurried towards the bridal group. His eyes met Kambi's. It was as magical and profound as it had been on the plateau. This was another sign. He couldn't possibly live without her.

Kambi alighted from the Jeep and shut the door. He held her hands, as she stared into his face.

"You came," she said, in a desperate rush to break the deafening silence between them.

"Yes," he replied, wondering how best to phrase his new proposition.

"Hi, Beba!" Kaycee yelled from the back seat of the car, swiping away the make-up artist's powder brush so she could wave.

"Congratulations!" Beba replied waving both hands. He walked towards the car and shook her outstretched hand.

"Thank you for coming. Kambi will be happier now," she said, "I'm sure of that."

Beba grinned when he caught the bride winking at Kambi, before she motioned the make-up artist to continue her task.

"I missed you so much it hurt," he said. Kambi frowned and turned away. "Believe me. I called several times, but you didn't answer. I thought you were still angry so I hid my number and called with a different number."

"So it was you," Kambi said.

"Yes." He paused and breathed deeply. "I found my mother but ..."

"You did? That's nice. But now's not a good time, Bee. I have to go back into the car. The bride is waiting."

"Life is short. I couldn't bear not to tell you that I thoroughly enjoyed your company and ..."

Her jaw dropped. He saw her eyes filling with tears

and knew that she felt something too. But what did she feel – fear or love, or both?

"We're already late for the reception. It'd be rude to keep the bride waiting," Kambi said, as she turned towards the car. "Let's talk later."

In a swift movement, Beba swung her around and kissed her. Then, he released her. Gasping, she climbed in the car, whipped out one of the souvenir notepads and said, "Take this. See you at the Marina Resort for the reception."

Beba nodded. He watched as the car went through the church gates. *Would she give an open-ended answer?* His heart beat faster as his driver pulled up beside him. Beba climbed into his car and handed the driver the notepad.

"Marina Resort?" the driver asked, peering into the rear-view mirror.

"Yes."

While the car drove past the U.J. Esuene Stadium and turned into more tree-lined streets, Beba remembered the first time he'd driven through similar roads, arguing about African print material. He replayed their arguments in his mind and got so carried away with his dreaming, he didn't notice when they arrived at the venue. He snapped out of his daydream, just as some young men gave instructions on how and where the driver could park his car. The men waved and saluted when they had finished explaining and went to help other guests.

Beba jumped down from the car and said, "You might

not need to wait for me. Watch me. I'll give you a thumbs up if I want you to give me the keys and leave."

"Otherwise?" the driver asked.

Beba sighed. "I hope to God I give you a thumbs up."

The couple were already having their photographs taken. Veil in hand, Kambi stood on the side, cheering them on with words like 'smile' and 'say cheese'. He stared long and hard at her until she turned and their eyes locked.

They sneaked out of view, behind the flowers, in the middle of another garden near the Slave History Museum. They stopped and stared, as though their eyes had said it all. A breeze from the lake cooled their faces. Beba took her hand.

"My mother has Alzheimer's, she's lost most of her memory. Occasionally, she becomes conscious and half-aware of her surroundings," he said, peering into her eyes.

She nodded. "Did you speak to her? Did she know who you were?"

"She doesn't even remember the children she raised. So I couldn't pour out my heart as I'd planned," he said. "But she kept staring and calling me Beba, also my father's name. She remembers my father, I think."

"That's sad," said Kambi. "So what do you do now?"

"What can I do? Pray? Live and love as though each day is my last?"

"It's surprising to hear a rich, handsome man talk about misery and the ephemeral nature of life."

"Money isn't everything. And you know, when my mother wasn't calling me Beba, the Nigerian student, she was telling me other truths. Once, while her son went to call a nurse, she said something shocking: 'Don't just exist: live.' Then she gave my hand a reassuring squeeze and smiled." Beba seemed rather excited.

"That's profound. So, how do you intend to live?"

"First, I shall tell the most beautiful woman I ever met that I have fallen for her," he said.

Beba's heart pounded faster. *Will she give us a chance? Will I go home aching inside?*

Kambi tilted her head to the left and said, "Is there someone new, Beba? How nice of you to tell me – out of respect for our friendship – about your new relationship."

"Oh, please let me finish," Beba said. Kambi's interjections were making him stutter.

"Bravo," she added, clearing her throat, as though she was bracing herself for the news. "You met someone new? A real fiancée, right?"

"Candy ... sorry, Kambi. Can I call you Candy, please?" She nodded, waved him on. He saw that she was anxious to hear about the unannounced object of his affection.

"Candy," he started and they heard the master of ceremonies call for the maid of honour.

"The couple needs toast glasses," a woman called. "Kambi, remember you have to make a toast. The bride said you owe her a poem!"

Kambi touched Beba's arm and ran off. "I am dying to hear about her ... but duty calls. Sorry."

"But, before you go, I have to tell you this: I cannot imagine a future without you. Since you left, you've stayed in my mind. I'm in love, Candy. With you."

Her eyes widened in disbelief. She leaped into his arms and pushed her nose into his cheek. Beba felt her shiver as though every fibre in her body had awakened with sparks. Her breathing spoke of her longing for him. Beba realised this and heard her body and soul calling out to him. He kissed her gently. His tenderness brought a smile to her lips. She sighed, rubbed her nose against his.

"Kambi, maid of honour! Toast time!" the master of ceremonies called, again.

"I have to go," she said, as he released his grip. Smoothing her dress, she stepped back and blew him a kiss before disappearing behind a hibiscus and ixora bush.

Pumping his fist in the air, Beba mouthed a triumphant "Yes!"

"She loves me too," he said, looking up to the heavens. "Can you believe my good fortune?"

He turned and saw his driver sitting among the other guests with his arms folded across his chest. And Beba gave him a thumbs up.

Kambi was standing behind the microphone, smiling. Bending slightly, she spoke into the microphone: "A toast to Tonye and Kaycee, because you understand the machinations of love." She paused, closed her eyes and spoke softly to the rhythm of the jazz melody.

Don't ask me how I know.
My heart never lies.
Even though it sleeps safely in your care,
In trust.
Love knows how itself to show,
Even in the dark, it glows,
And when we're apart, it grows,
In trust.

A round of applause interrupted her recital. She smiled, spotted Beba in the crowd, and blew him a kiss.

And with every ounce of energy in him he blew her a kiss back.

Once they'd popped open the bottles of champagne, Kambi walked up to Beba with two glasses.

"Cheers!" she cooed. Beba nodded, clinking glasses.

"To love and happiness!"

"To love and happiness!" Kambi said. She finished her champagne in one gulp and pulled Beba onto the dance floor.

While they swayed and dipped and glided, Kambi put her hands around his neck.

"Today has been great for me. Extraordinary, in fact." Kambi heart's swelled with joy. She wished her sister had been here to meet him. *If only Diana hadn't had to travel for that training at her office ...*

"Of course, you should be happy. You're maid of honour. Second-in-command after the bride."

Kambi threw her head back and laughed, "Not just that. My agent phoned this morning to tell me she'd got another offer for my poetry collection."

"That's wonderful news. Congratulations!"

"But that's not the best. The man who makes me feel high has just told me he's in love with me."

Beba pulled back while she twirled around to the music.

"I'll never leave your side," he said. He did a moonwalk around her. "Say you'll spend the rest of your life with me."

"For real?"

"Yes. This time I'm for real."

***

Kambi danced with her hands up in the air, even though every muscle in her body ached. Beba was too excited to remember his half-burned vineyard or the other setbacks Kems Industries was facing. They had cast all their troubles behind and were celebrating their love. Making the most of their time together was more important than anything else.

Kaycee walked up to them. She had changed into a halter-neck red evening gown and was holding a glass of champagne. "You've both been dancing since noon," she said, laughing. "Too bad Diana missed all this fun." She had to scream above the din of the music for Kambi to hear her.

"Yes. How sad. She called this morning and asked me to send her pictures. She was almost in tears," Kambi said, smiling. "And there's so much to celebrate."

Beba nodded. He was doing a rumba.

Kambi looked at him and felt her heart fill with pride. "We're leaving, Tonye and I are leaving," Kaycee said, waving her hands in the direction of the car park.

Kambi held her hand and said, "Have a beautiful honeymoon."

"Thank you. I'll be in touch," she replied. Then she turned to Beba and said, "Take care of my friend."

Beba laughed and said, "I will do my best to care for Miss I-prefer-to-do-things-myself. I love her the way she is, though."

Kambi playfully punched him in the shoulder. He winced and hugged her. Kambi laughed so hard her ribs ached. She hoped too much happiness didn't have side-effects. Her cheeks were already aching.

"Kaycee," Tonye hugged her from behind and said, "Time to go."

He was tall and dark-skinned; a contrast to Kaycee who was light-skinned and short.

He exchanged friendly handshakes with Beba and hugged Kambi. "Thank you for coming," Tonye said. "We really appreciate your presence and your presents."

Kambi nodded her acceptance. Beba said, "You're welcome."

Kambi leaned on Beba's chest and stared as the couple